THE WRONG WAY DOWN

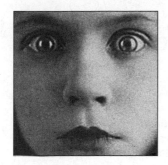

THE WRONG
WAY DOWN

Elizabeth Daly

FELONY & MAYHEM PRESS • NEW YORK

All the characters and events portrayed in this work are fictitious.

THE WRONG WAY DOWN

A Felony & Mayhem mystery

PRINTING HISTORY
First edition (Rinehart): 1946
Felony & Mayhem edition: 2013

ISBN: 978-1-937384-73-9

Manufactured in the United States of America

Printed on 100% recycled paper

Library of Congress Cataloging-in-Publication Data

Daly, Elizabeth, 1878-1967.
   The wrong way down / Elizabeth Daly. -- Felony & Mayhem edition
      pages cm
   1. Gamadge, Henry (Fictitious character)--Fiction. 2. New York (N.Y.)--
Fiction. 3. Bibliographers--Fiction. I. Title.
   PS3507.A4674W75 2013
   813'.54--dc23
                                    2013004155

CONTENTS

The icon above says you're holding a copy of a book in the Felony & Mayhem "Vintage" category. These books were originally published prior to about 1965, and feature the kind of twisty, ingenious puzzles beloved by fans of Agatha Christie and John Dickson Carr. If you enjoy this book, you may well like other "Vintage" titles from Felony & Mayhem Press.

For more about these books, and other Felony & Mayhem titles, or to place an order, please visit our website at:

www.FelonyAndMayhem.com

Other "Vintage" titles from

FELONY&MAYHEM

THE WRONG WAY DOWN

CHAPTER ONE

Two Front Doors

IT MIGHT HAVE been an empty house. The windows were all shuttered, the columns on either side of the small portico were defaced by scribblings in red chalk and pencil, the white front door needed a coat of paint. Dust, and dead leaves from one of the little trees that struggled for existence along the avenue, had blown against the sill, which was almost flush with the street.

The house seemed to have two front entrances, one above the other; a not uncommon sight even on Park Avenue since the days when all these dwellings had lost their high stoops in the interests of city development. They had been remodeled in various ways, and this house in the quickest, cheapest and easiest way—by constructing a new front door in place of a basement window, closing up the old storm doors above, and placing an ornamental rail around the old original doorstep; thus simulating a little balcony.

Gamadge, looking up at the dark front windows in the twilight of the December afternoon, guessed that Miss

1

Paxton, temporarily residing there as a sort of honorary agent and caretaker, used back rooms for the sake of quiet. But he reflected, looking up and down the avenue, that this was as quiet a stretch as you could find in New York; far uptown, with private houses—some of them empty—on both sides of the way.

This house would soon be really empty too; empty and for sale. Miss Paxton, as described to Gamadge by his wife, wasn't the kind of old lady who would approve of neglect and dinginess, but perhaps she didn't feel like spending the owner's money on outdoor work for the short time she would be living here, and she herself had very little money of her own to spend on anything.

He looked at his watch. Almost five o'clock, time for his call. He wasn't to ring, he remembered; Miss Paxton had said over the telephone that she would leave the front door on the latch for him. She didn't much like stairs, and the daily woman was deaf.

He had protested a little over this arrangement, but she had sensibly asked him who would know that that particular door was going to be on the latch for an hour on that Tuesday afternoon? Did sneak thieves, even in New York, go up and down all day trying door knobs? He had agreed with her that they probably didn't, but he had privately wished that she had somebody with her in the house besides a part-time char.

Miss Julia Paxton, an old friend of his wife's family, was a resident of Tarrytown. Of late years she had come very seldom to New York. She had called up that morning to tell the Gamadges that she was in town closing up a house for some Western relatives, and that she would like very much to see Clara again, and to meet Clara's husband. All her old friends in New York had died or gone away, and she didn't know anybody there but the Gamadges any more. Clara was South, and Gamadge had thought it only decent to pay the call himself.

He opened the door, locked the latch, and shut himself into a dark, bare hallway. There was a closed door to his right, a closed door at the farther end of the passage, and a stairway on his left. This had been the basement once, but money had been spent on it, at least, after the remodeling; the floor was laid in gray mosaic, and the walls handsomely papered in gray and gold.

As he reached the foot of the stairs the part-time woman began to descend them, laden with brushes, mop and pail. She saw Gamadge, peered at him through the gloom, and stood aside for him to pass. A person too deaf to answer doorbells shows no interest in visitors—they are not her job. A long-faced, sallow, elderly creature, with wisps of gray hair over her forehead and the hedged-in look of the deaf, she stood as if stooped with the exhaustion of the day's end. Her working dress conformed to the stoop by rising in the back to show a dismal inch of slip or petticoat.

Gamadge said loudly: "Miss Paxton expects me."

"What say?"

"Miss Paxton expects me."

"Yes, sir? First floor back."

Gamadge passed her, getting an aroma of soap and metal polish. Questionable indeed, he thought, would any shape have to be in order to get a challenge from the cleaning woman.

The hall light went on, and a pleasant old voice greeted him from the landing:

"Mr. Gamadge, this *is* nice of you. I'm sorry I let you come in into the dark, but I never remember how little light there is in a city house."

Gamadge shook hands with Miss Paxton, who was very trim in a black-and-white print dress. He said: "It was nice of you to call up. Clara will be awfully sorry to miss you, but she and the infant had a touch of flu, and I made her take him South for the cold weather."

"I haven't seen her for years; such a lovely girl." She led the way across a hall hung with pictures, into a large back room that had a look of being more formal than its furniture. Its shutters were closed, and a round table between the windows held a shaded lamp; it also held writing materials, books and magazines, Miss Paxton's handbag, her workbag, and a heap of knitting.

"Do sit down and make yourself comfortable." Miss Paxton indicated a chair opposite her own, beside which was a little table set out with a decanter and glasses. The glasses were sherry glasses; a cake basket held cakes and cookies.

"I want to look at you." Settled in her chair, she fixed a friendly gaze on him through steel spectacles. Gamadge, returning the gaze, saw an alert wrinkled face, perceptive blue eyes. She saw a thinnish, tallish, green-eyed man of forty who looked amiable.

"Well!" said Miss Paxton. "So this is Clara Dawson's husband. She wrote me that you had a beautiful disposition."

"So has she. That's why we married each other."

"People don't marry for such sensible reasons. She didn't tell me much about your little boy."

"She couldn't; the child's indescribable. Has a thoughtful expression when he looks at you that I don't half like." Gamadge glanced about him. "You seem very comfortable here, Miss Paxton."

"I am, very. James Ashbury—that's the second cousin who now owns the house, you know—wrote me that I was to treat the place as if it were my own. Well, I sent him all the wine and spirits that were in the cellar, but I took the liberty of using up what was opened and in the sideboard. Do have some sherry—it's very good. Pour a glass for me and for yourself, and help yourself to cake."

Gamadge did as he was told.

"I hope you don't depend on tea in the afternoon," said Miss Paxton. "I never did drink it."

Gamadge, handing her her glass and the cake basket, said that sherry was just what he needed.

When they were both served he asked how long she had been in town.

"I came the week after Thanksgiving, November twenty-eighth. I closed up my little old house in Tarrytown and came down for the winter—it will take me a long time to get this job done. I'm getting rid of all the things James didn't want sent out to him in California, you know. At least I'm going to get rid of them."

"How lucky he was to persuade you to do such a complicated, tiresome thing."

"I'm the lucky one." Miss Paxton sipped sherry. "I've always been very intimate with the family, especially with my cousin Lawson, James' father, who owned the house and died here last Spring. I really know the place, and the things in it. I shall enjoy the work. Such a nice change, too, and a warm, comfortable city house. And I go to the movies; right around the corner, or almost. Oh, I'm having quite a holiday."

The cleaning woman appeared at the arched entrance from the hall. She was now wearing a large felt hat perched high on her head, and an ulster which had seen better days and was a little short for her. She said: "Excuse me, Miss Paxton, I'm going now. Do you want me to pick up anything for you on my way here tomorrow?"

"No, thank you, Mrs. Keate," said Miss Paxton, in an amiable shout.

The cleaning woman turned and went across the hall to the stairs.

Gamadge said: "I hope she's here with you all day. I wish she were with you at night, too."

"Oh dear no; from three to five except Saturdays and Sundays. I was fortunate to get *any*one. It's very hard to find these part-time persons."

"So Clara says."

"I got this one because she used to work for Cousin Lawson. I'm lucky in every way. The furnace man next door attends to my garbage, which doesn't amount to anything, because I go out to little restaurants for lunch and dinner. Breakfast of course is nothing. Really it's quite like Heaven for a change, living in New York."

"I'm glad you find it so."

"I shop, I go to the museums. I'm thoroughly enjoying myself. And it's an oil furnace, I can run it. Like magic, after my old thing in Tarrytown."

"You must come to dinner with me some night soon."

"How very nice of you. I should love to. At present I'm quite busy on lists and writing to dealers. I got James' things off to him yesterday."

"Don't you find yourself rather tired of an evening? I should be fit for a week in hospital after one of your days."

"Of course I don't get tired!" Miss Paxton denied the possibility with vigor. "I suggested doing the work myself. James only asked me to stay here and superintend—he couldn't come East, he's very busy and he has a delicate wife. Do smoke."

Gamadge lighted a cigarette.

"The insurance people and the real estate agent recommended appraisers and dealers," continued Miss Paxton, "and I'm writing to them. I'm very anxious to get good prices for things. James doesn't expect much, and I should like to surprise him. He has the best things, of course—rugs, paintings, furniture. He picked them out from the inventory I sent him."

"Don't sell the chairs from under yourself."

"I've got a funny collection of things in here, haven't I?" Miss Paxton looked about her with amusement. "From all over the house. This was the dining room, and there's a splendid pantry behind you there with a little electric stove and an icebox. So convenient. I live in these two rooms—this and the one just above it, the bedroom that used to be Cousin Lawson's and Cousin Marietta's. I like having only one flight of stairs to climb, as I have at home; and I don't climb that more than I have to. Just a little stiffness."

"Mr. Ashbury was a very lucky man to find such an agent."

"I have every reason for obliging that family. I'll tell you why, and you must tell Clara—she'll be interested, because it's always been well known among my friends that I never had more than enough to be barely comfortable on." Miss Paxton sat back, glass in hand, and looked at Gamadge with a kind of incredulity. "Cousin Lawson Ashbury left me three thousand a year in his will. I'm to have it for life."

"That's splendid news, Miss Paxton."

"He and dear Marietta were friends, aside from being cousins; but he needn't have done it. It's like a fairy tale. Three thousand a year! Why, with what I have of my own, I need never worry at all about getting really old and needing people to take care of me. I'm only seventy-five," she told him gaily, "I might go on for twenty years. My grandmother did."

"With all that income you might consider having a regular maid here to live in and wait on you."

"Henry Gamadge, do you know what that would cost here in New York?"

"Well, yes; I do."

"I shan't spend my money like that, I assure you! I shall save it for later on, when I might need a practical nurse," she informed him with some severity. "Do you know what a practical nurse costs?"

"Well, yes. I just thought it might be pleasanter for you not to be all alone at night."

"I'm alone at night when I'm at home, and I haven't neighbors on all sides of me in the country. No, this is the time to save. And I'm particularly anxious to show James my appreciation, because he and his family were so nice about my having the trust fund. Why, just think—at three per cent the capital would be a hundred thousand dollars."

"A lot of money."

"I should think so. And James sent his and his wife's congratulations, they really sounded pleased. He can hardly remember me, he went West when he was so young a man, so long ago. He has two children, a son and a daughter, whom I've never seen, and this second wife. Really I'm very glad that he's a successful man with plenty of money of his own.

If he wasn't I might be conscience-stricken. Nearly a third of the estate! Another third went to Cousin Lawson's church, and the rest, and this house, to James. But what can James do with this house? They tell me it's worth very little as it is, and the other houses in the row aren't for sale, so nobody can buy them and put up an apartment. And it costs so much to remodel into flats."

"Don't lose sleep over Mr. James Ashbury."

"There's somebody else I do worry about a little."

"Who's that?"

Miss Paxton frowned at her thoughts. "Cousin Lawson had one other relative—a great-niece named Iris Vance. Her parents are dead, and except for the Ashburys she seems to be quite alone in the world. But Cousin Lawson didn't leave her anything at all."

"Why not?"

"There was a family quarrel, if you could call it that."

"And Mr. Ashbury deceased took it out on this girl?"

"She was in it. The quarrel was on account of her."

"Something she did?"

"And she was only ten years old at the time. Still..." Miss Paxton sat twirling her sherry glass, a peculiar look of doubt and distaste in her eye. "Her father and mother always seemed such cultivated, pleasant people, too. I never could understand it. I knew them quite well; they used to come here long ago when I was staying in the house, and we'd all go to the theatre; Iris' mother used to come here, of course, long before she was married. It was all so cheerful and gay in those days. I can see us going down the front steps—the stoop wasn't gone then—to the carriage or the car, on our way to some theatre. The Ashburys were always giving us treats."

"What turned out to be the matter with the Vances?" asked Gamadge, who was sitting back and idly smoking.

"The Ashburys always knew that the Vances were devout spiritualists. That wasn't the trouble, although Lawson and Marietta didn't approve. Mr. Vance was an artist, so well-bred and agreeable; his wife seemed flighty to me, but pleasant too. They weren't mediums themselves, you know, just devout believers.

"But that poor little Iris! Brought up to it, taking it all for granted, and encouraged when she was supposed to develop what they called psychic gifts. She was a medium from babyhood! It just made it all too horrible. Not for money, you know, but somehow that makes it worse—more *real*."

"The parents exploited her?"

"They didn't call it that, they said it would be criminal to suppress her powers. They were never allowed to mention the subject to the Ashburys. They came here on the understanding that it never must be mentioned."

"What was the little girl like?"

"A very pretty red-haired child, always dressed in white, and with something so eerie about her. As if she were living on a different plane from ours, a much higher one, and knew things we couldn't know. Really, a most annoying little thing, though she never said anything impertinent. Very good manners."

"Hard to live with," agreed Gamadge. "Tough on the unbelievers."

"But that wouldn't have alienated the Ashburys, who were the kindest people. But one day when her parents brought her here to call with them—she made something happen."

"What?" Gamadge was interested.

"The Ashburys never would say. They avoided the whole subject, and the Vances never came here again."

"Drastic."

"I ought to explain that that kind of thing would seem much more serious to Cousin Lawson and Cousin Marietta than to most people, because they thought that mediums *can* make things happen, but only through the agency of evil spirits. And it happened in the drawing room," said Miss Paxton, glancing at the partition wall to her right.

"That makes it bad," said Gamadge. "Evil spirits in the drawing room."

"And invoked by a child! I mean in the middle of tea," explained Miss Paxton, "and the parents delighted. Until, of course, Cousin Marietta fainted. It nearly killed her. She was in bed a week. Do you really wonder so much that Cousin Lawson wouldn't leave any of the Vances money to be spent on such things? But I'm afraid they weren't well off, and when I had the news about my legacy and found that Iris Vance wasn't getting a penny—well, I made up my mind to get in touch with her. When I got to town this Fall I looked her up—she's in the telephone book. I asked her to call, and she came last Sunday."

"What's she like now?"

"A pretty girl, I'm sure anybody would call her that, with beautiful red hair and a fair skin. But her features are not clear-cut; there's a blurriness about them. More like a picture than a person," said Miss Paxton.

"A French modern portrait?" Gamadge looked pleased at her description. "A Laurencin?"

"Well, yes."

"Subtle, perhaps?"

"That's the very word."

"Did you like her? I don't think you did."

"I had determined to like her, and to—well—you know; find out how she was situated financially. She shocked me inexpressibly by telling me that she was a professional medium now, and making an excellent living by it."

"Really."

"And she seemed proud of it. I couldn't help feeling that in her own sly way she was laughing at me all the time."

"These adepts. Did she say what branch of the profession she particularly went in for? Crystal gazing, polite palmistry? Or is she a regular trance medium, with all the trimmings? There's a lot of difference."

"I didn't ask."

"There's one thing I hope you did ask."

Miss Paxton laughed in spite of herself. "I asked her what happened in the drawing room that day—I couldn't help it."

"But she wouldn't say?"

"Henry Gamadge, I could have shaken her; she said she was in trance at the time and didn't know!"

"I *would* have shaken her. Here I'm dying of curiosity."

"So am I. Do you know what I've sometimes thought? Only you couldn't think it of her father and mother."

"What?"

"That they put her up to it, whatever it was, to try to convince Cousin Lawson and Cousin Marietta and get them into the fold!"

"Well, after all, that's just the kind of thing fanatical persons are accused of doing from the highest motives."

After a pause Miss Paxton asked: "There's a good deal of so-called evidence for that kind of thing, isn't there?"

"For spiritualistic manifestations? Oceans of it." He added: "If you study it you may find yourself in the fold before you know where you are. The human mind is fearfully and wonderfully made."

"I shan't study it. But...will you laugh?"

"At anything you seriously tell me? Certainly not."

"Since she was here something else has happened—or I think it has. And I can't help wondering whether she made it happen, just to show me she could."

Gamadge sat up. "What on earth do you mean?"

"Of course I'm not young, and I do forget things now and then."

"Not as many things as I do, I'd be willing to bet on it."

"I'm so sure about this." Miss Paxton rose. "Will you just let me tell you about it in my own way?"

"Any way you like."

She stood looking at him oddly. "I think I'd better lead up to it. I shouldn't like you to think my brain is going."

"I'll bet against that, too."

"Clara wrote me that you liked mysteries."

"I do, very much."

"If you can just explain this without bringing the spirits into it!"

"However I explain it, if I explain it at all, the spirits won't be the explanation."

"You're so comforting."

She went in front of him across the room and into the hall, which was carpeted in red and lighted by tulip-shaped globes set in the gilt foliage of the wall brackets. Gamadge's eyes wandered over the pictures—framed etchings, engravings, an old-fashioned water color or two that looked as if someone in the family had had a little talent for sketching.

"James doesn't want any of these," said Miss Paxton. "He wouldn't let me send him an itemized list. He's sure they're almost worthless. But he's never properly seen them at all, he admits it; and I'm getting the right people to look at them, of course."

"At first glance I'm inclined to agree with him that there won't be much of value found here. One or two of the engravings, perhaps…"

"Cousin Lawson and his father liked to buy pictures of places they visited abroad, and reproductions of paintings they liked in the galleries. There are more in the book-room. I haven't been through those cupboards yet." Miss Paxton, who had turned to the left after they came out of the dining room, stood with her eyes fixed on an engraving which hung just above the level of her eyes. "Will you look at this one?"

CHAPTER TWO

The Lady Audley

GAMADGE MOVED TO Miss Paxton's side and looked at the engraving, which was framed in black and gold. He said: "Now that might be a nice little value. It's a good copperplate. Who's it a portrait of? Let's see: 'The Lady Audley.'"

"Cousin Lawson's father, my Uncle Vincent, bought it because he thought it looked like his wife. Will you take it down and bring it into the sitting room, please, and tell me all you can about it?"

"You mean describe it as if for an inventory?"

"If you can."

"It tells a good deal about itself; I could add a little more, perhaps."

He lifted it off its hook and carried it into the sitting room. Miss Paxton cleared a space for it on her table, and he laid it face upward in the full light of the lamp.

"We have here," said Gamadge, "an aquatint engraving—"

"What's an aquatint?" asked Miss Paxton, who stood

beside him with a look of intense interest on her troubled face.

"An engraving etched on copperplate with aqua fortis— nitric acid. Etched in what you might call a dotty way—with dots instead of lines. By the way, it isn't very dusty. Good housekeeping here."

Miss Paxton looked surprised and amused.

"Etched on pink paper," continued Gamadge.

"Pink?"

"Pinkish, what they call pink. It's eighteenth century— I'm not cheating, I haven't looked at the inscription yet—and a good deal older than its frame. It was engraved by a master. It's a portrait—head and shoulders—of a lady in the costume and headdress of the first half of the sixteenth century. She is not exactly beautiful, but she has a delicate, highbred face, and by the cut of the mouth alone I should say she had been painted by Holbein. Shall I go on to the lettering?"

"Please," said Miss Paxton in a dry voice.

Gamadge read aloud:

THE LADY AUDLEY
From the original by Hans Holbein
Engraved by F. BARTOLOZZI, Historical Engraver to His Majesty
Published as the Act directs Oct. 1, 1793
By I. Chamberlaine

"His Majesty," remarked Gamadge, looking up at Miss Paxton, "must have been King George the Third. Bartolozzi— who *was* a master—seems to have been engaged by this Chamberlaine to engrave a series of portraits for a book. What series? Well, Holbein painted portraits of court ladies and gentlemen for King Henry the Eighth. Lady Audley must have been one of them, and at some time or other one of the books was looted of its portraits—often occurs."

"Very interesting indeed," said Miss Paxton, still dryly.

"My cousin Lawson always said he wished he knew who the portrait was of."

"You mean he wished he knew who Lady Audley was?"

"No. He didn't know it was a portrait of Lady Audley."

"But—" Gamadge, puzzled, ran his finger along the glass at the bottom of the picture—"it says *Lady Audley* here, in letters a quarter of an inch high."

"Yes. Now I'll tell *you* something interesting: Until yesterday evening, when I looked at that picture closely for the first time in some years, there has not been one word of writing on it. Not one word."

Gamadge straightened himself, looked down at her, and asked mildly: "No letters?"

"Letters? No writing. I have looked at it often in the past, because as I said it was supposed to resemble Cousin Lawson's mother, of course in youth. I never saw the resemblance myself, but I only remembered my aunt as a middle-aged woman. I hadn't looked at it closely since I came here two weeks ago, but I looked at it. It was just as it has always been. And then on Sunday evening, after I finished a letter to a picture dealer, I came out into the hall with my pad and pencil to make a sort of list of all these pictures. It had developed the inscription. Well, I'm not a nervous woman."

"Evidently not." Gamadge took out his cigarette case, lighted a cigarette, looked down at Lady Audley, and said: "For Heaven's sake."

"I could almost swear it was blank on Saturday."

"Was the light on in the hall then?"

"I don't remember; I should think not, since it was morning. But I'd have noticed all that." She glanced at the inscription below the portrait and away again.

"Very unlikely that you should be mistaken. It was as always on Saturday. The cleaning woman doesn't come on Saturday or Sunday, but on Sunday Miss Vance called on you; Miss Vance, who makes things happen."

"I couldn't help wondering—"

"I can't help wondering either. Of course it would be more satisfactory if we were absolutely certain that the picture was as usual before Miss Vance came. Could Mr. Ashbury in California settle that for us?"

"I don't think so. He's not been East since he settled in San Francisco as a young man, and he wasn't at all the kind of boy to be interested in such things. Cousin Lawson mentioned the resemblance of the portrait to his mother because I'd known his mother; James never knew his grandmother at all. But I could write to James—if necessary. If not, I shouldn't much like to."

"The picture isn't fully described in any inventory that you know of?"

"No, the insurance inventory lumps all the small pictures together as a 'lot.'"

"And so your only evidence that the picture changed," said Gamadge, smiling at her, "is at present the evidence of your own eyes."

"And my memory. I don't think I'm mistaken."

"A mystery, quite a mystery." Gamadge bent to study the face of Lady Audley. "You know, this name seems to attract mystery. There was a nice old shocker by Miss Braddon—*Lady Audley's Secret.*"

"I dimly remember the title."

"Nothing but a murder; Lady Audley's secret, if I remember it, was only that she pushed somebody down a well. Nothing to *this.* This is much subtler, much creepier altogether. I wonder if we could make it less creepy."

"I wish we could."

"But it might still be disagreeable, you know."

"It couldn't be as disagreeable as having to believe that Iris Vance can make words come out on a framed picture more than a hundred years old."

"Framed." Gamadge repeated the word in a tone that sounded inquiring. He turned the aquatint. "Well, this is gratifying, I must say."

"What is?"

"Not a professional job, the framing."

"No, I remember that Uncle Vincent wanted to frame it, and found one in the house that just fitted. And I remember what used to be in this old black and gold thing—one of those dreadful memorials made out of hair."

"Hair?"

"And seaweed and shells. Somebody's hair was the weeping willow over the tombstone."

"That's a new one on me," said Gamadge admiringly. "Better than framing the funeral wreath." He was gently fiddling with the wooden back of the frame, and the old nails.

"Well, Uncle Vincent had the sense to throw the thing away."

Gamadge turned Lady Audley face upwards again. He asked: "Any reference books in that book-room you spoke of? Dictionaries of names?"

"There must be. It's only a large closet off the drawing room, you know, with cupboards under the shelves for pictures."

"Lead me to it. I'd like to find out something more about Lady Audley, if I can." He added, as they went along the hall to the front of the house, "The Ashburys could have found out something about Lady Audley if they'd wanted to."

"You mean the book would be here—the book the picture came out of?"

"Oh, no; why should Ashbury mutilate his own book? The portrait was out of the book when he bought it, I'm sure. I mean he could have taken the portrait to a dealer."

"Well, you know how people are; they wonder and wonder and don't do a thing."

"Restful."

Miss Paxton opened a door at right angles to the old storm doors, and switched on lights. Gamadge saw a high amber-colored room with a parquet floor; gilt, brocaded furniture was huddled together at the window end. She went to a door in the opposite wall, and opened it. Gamadge followed her into a little room walled with books; below them, handles were set into broad panels of wood.

Gamadge turned slowly from shelf to shelf. "A nice, solid lot," he said. "Speeches. Travels. Lives. A little fiction in its nobler form—Scott, George Eliot. All in fine condition."

"I'm afraid the Ashburys weren't great readers."

"Dealers hate great readers—you'll get good money for this little library. Let's see—nothing here for us, unless that dictionary of names." He pulled out a big volume. "Audley, Audley, Audley. Lots of Audleys, but no Lady Audleys, and nothing to say which Audley we want." He replaced the dictionary.

Miss Paxton tugged at one of the handles: "Here's where the loose pictures are. These funny tip-out cupboards; like bins."

A panel came out from the wall to the extent of about a foot, and stopped. Gamadge turned to glance into the mass of photographs, engravings and sheet music within.

"Of course I'll have them all gone over," said Miss Paxton.

Gamadge separated the mass here and there. "Plenty of colored photographs," he said. "Very nice ones."

"Some of the things Cousin Lawson or his father picked up in the galleries abroad."

Gamadge pushed the cupboard to. "We'll have to telephone."

"Telephone?"

"To a man I know who might know about Lady Audley."

"The telephone is on the landing of the back stairs." Miss Paxton led the way with alacrity. "I must say I like people who get things done."

"I hope I'll catch him in his office where he keeps his files."

"Would he be in his office at this time of day?"

"Hall practically lives in his office. He's always talking about retiring, but he hates to get far away from his books."

They went through a door at the back of the hall to the landing of the service stairs. Miss Paxton insisted on his sitting on the stool in front of the telephone shelf, while she stood at his elbow. He dialed.

"Hall? This is Gamadge. I'm asking a favor as usual. A little information about a picture in a book, it's rather urgent." He winked at Miss Paxton, who winked back at him. "The book is a collection of Holbein portraits engraved by Bartolozzi and published by I. Chamberlaine in 1793... Of course you know it. The picture I'm interested in is one of Lady Audley: A for Audley, U for urgent, D for—all right. I simply want to know who she was...You have? That's wonderful. Just a minute; when you call me back, call me at—" Gamadge looked at the number below the dial and repeated it twice. "Thanks, Hall. I'll be right here."

He put down the receiver and swung to look up at Miss Paxton. "We're lucky. Hall has a catalogue of a sale, he has millions of them. It's itemized. He's sure there's a description of the book in it, with the plates fully described too."

"Why," said Miss Paxton, "it's the simplest thing in the world to find out about pictures, isn't it?"

"Simplest thing in the world," agreed Gamadge.

"Just ask the right person."

"That's all."

"But I must confess I don't know why you should go to the trouble. Neither of us cares exactly who she was, do we? And it would have been enough for Uncle Vincent just to know what it says on the picture—now."

"There's method in what I'm doing," said Gamadge. "I had to supply Hall with details about the aquatint; as I couldn't do it, I'm making him supply them himself." He turned on his bench to look along the hallway. "I rather wish you had the telephone nearer you at night. It's not even on the same floor as your bedroom. Now wait a minute: I know you're only seventy-five, but anybody can have acute indigestion in the small hours. I'm going to leave you the address of my doctor; he's a young fellow, doesn't mind being called at night."

"It's very kind of you, Henry. I don't have indigestion, but it's very kind indeed of you."

"And I beg that you won't leave that front door on the latch as you did today."

"I never did before, and I won't again." She added: "Burglars would be a little disappointed. I have only this gold brooch I wear, and my two old rings, and my watch. And I never keep much money in the house."

"Nothing disappoints burglars."

The telephone rang. Gamadge snatched up the receiver. "Yes, Hall? You have? Fine. Wait till I get out my pencil… *Elizabeth, daughter of Sir Brian Tuke. Married George Touchet, Lord Audley*…Not the chancellor; I see; the other one. Well, Hall, I'm more than grateful. Oh, by the way— what figures would you quote on the aquatint?…I see. And how about proof before letter?…Yes, of course, I understand. Well, I can't say how much obliged I am. Hope you'll find something I can do for *you*. Good-bye."

He put down the receiver and sat looking up at Miss Paxton and smiling.

"Well!" She returned his smile. "We know all about her now. We even know that her husband wasn't the chancellor."

"We know more than that. Tell me, Miss Paxton: did Miss Vance have an opportunity to examine this Audley portrait on Sunday?"

"Why, I suppose she may have glanced at it as she came into the sitting room with me. It was just beyond the door, as you know."

"How about later, when she went home? Did you see her out?"

"She wouldn't hear of it. I stayed in the sitting room."

"Could you *hear* her go out?"

"Hear her? Why, no; the carpets are thick, and the front door doesn't slam if you don't absolutely crash it."

"She may have seen this picture in her childhood, when she came here with her parents?"

"I suppose so."

"Her father was an artist. She may have learned something of art, engravings, that kind of thing from him?"

"Yes." Miss Paxton was gazing at him fixedly.

"One more question: that deaf charwoman of yours — she wouldn't be likely to let a stranger in, if she did happen to be in the front hall and hear the bell, without saying anything to you about it? She seemed rather casual to me."

"She can't *hear* the bell."

"And she wasn't here on Sunday. Well, Miss Paxton, I shouldn't worry about the spirits if I were you; reason maintains its sway."

"I'm very glad to hear it."

"We have every right to believe that your eyes didn't deceive you, that you never were mistaken, and that the portrait of Lady Audley never had a line of lettering on it until after Miss Vance left on Sunday afternoon. In fact, we have the makings of a very pretty little case against Miss Vance, though I'm afraid you won't see the beauty of it. Now for some more evidence."

He got up, put a hand on Miss Paxton's elbow, and steered her back into the sitting room. Picking up Lady Audley's portrait, he held it so that she could see the back of it.

"I said it wasn't dusty. That's because it's been handled within a very few days. These nails have been out recently." He laid the picture down again. "This engraving is what they call lettered proof. Did you ever hear of 'proof before letter'?"

"No."

"I thought not. And I think Miss Vance made a little money by her call on you last Sunday afternoon."

CHAPTER THREE

Proof Before Letter

MISS PAXTON SANK DOWN slowly in her chair. "I can see," she said, "that you think Iris Vance changed the pictures."

"If she did, she made money by it—or gave herself a chance to make money. The engraving that hung out there in the hall until—shall we say Sunday evening?"

"I'm sure I looked at it on Saturday morning."

"That engraving was a proof before letter; which means a proof impression carefully made from the finished plate before the printing of the ordinary issue—" he tapped the glass of the portrait before him—"and before any inscription whatever is added." He tapped the glass again, lower down. "Title, artist's name, engraver's name, date, anything."

Miss Paxton listened in silence.

"Proof before letter," continued Gamadge, "is more valuable than lettered proof. It's scarcer, for one thing, and it's often a finer impression. The engraver sometimes draws it himself. Now of course values differ very much from time to time in the case of things like this; fashions change, hobbies wax and wane, money is tight or free. Hall could only guess at these particular values—"

"That's why you asked him about the picture!"

"That's why. He guesses roughly that this impression we have before us now might be worth twenty-five to thirty dollars in the open market; but that a collector might pay a hundred for a proof before letter."

"Seventy dollars difference?"

"If you could find your market. In any case there'd be some difference, I should say fifty dollars at least. But Miss Vance, or anybody, would have to be prepared with the less valuable picture in order to make the change, and she'd have to be prepared with something else—information."

"You mean she knew she could make the change without being interfered with?"

"Certainly that." Gamadge stood contemplating Lady Audley biting the side of his thumb. He looked at Miss Paxton sideways. "You know these are not common."

"Lady Audleys?"

"I never saw her before in my life. Rather a coincidence for Miss Vance, for anybody who knew that there was one already in the house, to own or pick up another one. Most of them must be in the books, you know—the books they were engraved for. *All* the lettered ones would be in the books unless somebody tore one out. Do you know what I think, Miss Paxton?"

"I can't even imagine, Henry."

"I think this one must have been in the house too."

"Both of them in the house? I never heard that this one was."

"Well, it may have been, and your cousin Lawson Ashbury may never have heard of it either. It's an inferior copy of the portrait your uncle was interested in; let's say he acquired it first, and kept it in one of those tip-out receptacles in the book closet. Mr. Lawson Ashbury—did he live here all his life?"

"No, certainly not. He lived with Marietta in an apartment, or in the country."

"No reason why his father should keep him posted on all such purchases, was there?"

"None at all."

"Well, your uncle had this copy, and later on he found the finer one, the proof before letter. It was so fine and so much of an acquisition that he framed it and hung it in the hall. He'd lost interest in this one, never spoke of it to you or the rest of the family."

Miss Paxton said: "I can't for the life of me see why people shouldn't prefer the ones that have all the information on them."

"And you'd probably rather have a set of books in a handsome binding than in the original boards, uncut and unopened. Collectors wouldn't, no matter how fine the binding. And if you cut a page in one of their dratted Firsts, so as to read what the author said, they'd murder you.

"Well, we have the motive—malice, or a problematical seventy dollars. If we wanted to delve into psychology we might ask ourselves whether or not the very fact that the portrait resembled Mrs. Vincent Ashbury—"

"Henry, don't. It's too ugly."

"I told you you wouldn't see the beauty of the case. Now for opportunity. Miss Vance, as we have already seen, may have had opportunity to change the pictures after she supposedly left on Sunday afternoon. We presume that she understood the difference in value between letter proof and proof before letter. Can't we presume that when she was a child, a visitor in this house, she was allowed to poke about a little in the book-room? Look at the pictures there while her elders took their tea?"

"It's perfectly possible."

"If she was a practising medium at ten years old, her observation may have been sharpened and her natural childish liking for secrecy developed beyond the normal. She saw the picture—this picture—in the book closet; she knew it was almost a duplicate of the one in the hall; she said nothing: but she cashed in on that knowledge last Sunday afternoon."

"She was a precocious little thing, always asking questions about the curios and the bric-a-brac; but she was clever with her hands. They'd let her look at the pictures." Miss Paxton was frowning heavily. "She had a talent for drawing."

"There you are. She comes here—how many years later?"

"Fifteen. She says she's twenty-five now."

"She comes here, and as she enters this room she has a glimpse of the portrait of Lady Audley hanging where it always hung, just beyond this door. She wonders whether the other one is still in the book-room; she remembers that day long ago when she was perhaps detected in some hocus-pocus and disgraced; her parents with her. Lady Audley—there's a grimness about that Holbein look. If Mr. Lawson Ashbury's mother looked like that, and he looked like her, he could certainly be grim."

"Just serious, Henry. A charming man."

"But Miss Vance probably remembered one occasion when he was grim. After she leaves you, Miss Vance slips into the drawing room, into the book-room. You wouldn't have seen her from this chair of yours."

"As a matter of fact I was probably in the pantry; I always wash up the glasses as soon as—"

"Good, you were in the pantry. You wouldn't have seen her or heard her. She finds the other Lady Audley just where it used to be. Had you mentioned the fact that you didn't as yet know exactly what was in those tip-out cupboards?"

"Probably. We talked about what I was doing for James."

"And Miss Vance decides that nobody will ever miss the other Lady Audley, or notice a change. All the pictures in the hall are to be disposed of en bloc to a dealer. She doesn't know that *you* know what sentimental value your uncle attributed to the portrait. She's amused by the situation. She's used to taking chances, the great risks of her profession. She's clever with her hands, and she can move about like a ghost. She comes back past this doorway, takes the picture off its hook, takes it into the book cupboard, and makes the change. She has no tools, but she gets the nails back into the frame with the help of—what? Any small metal object that she finds in her handbag. She splinters the wood a little—rotten old wood. See?"

Miss Paxton leaned forward to gaze earnestly at the tiny splinters under one or two of the nails, and asked: "How did she pull them out?"

"Loosen them and you can pull them out with your fingers. She had something to do it with—perhaps a nail file—or she wouldn't have undertaken the job in the first place.

"She rolled the unlettered Lady Audley up, put it under her arm, having replaced it by this one. Then she went quietly down the stairs and out; and I'm sorry to tell you, Miss Paxton, that I think the other Lady Audley's gone forever."

"I really cannot bear it."

"Most irritating."

"To have allowed someone to walk off with James' property, under my very nose! It means that I'm not competent to do the work, that's all."

"Not competent? Miss Paxton! You've exposed the racket by your competence. You remembered something that most people would have forgotten, and you saw something that younger people mightn't have seen."

"That's very nice of you, Henry; but I feel responsible. I shall make it up to James, of course, but—oh, I do so wish we could prove all this, and let that girl know we'd proved it, and get the picture back. Is it really gone? Do you mean we couldn't trace it?"

"She wouldn't sell it in this neighborhood now; and even if she did, it would cost us more than seventy dollars to run it down. Nothing in that. As for your making up the money, isn't there burglary insurance?"

"But the insurance people would never pay any attention to such a story. They'd never pay. They'd say I was mistaken about everything."

"I was thinking that people of Miss Vance's profession don't like even the threat of court proceedings."

"Court proceedings?"

"If we had a case we could take it into court. We have the makings of one."

"That's what you said before. But—"

"One loophole for Miss Vance to crawl out of—somebody might have come into the house on Saturday or Sunday with a key."

"But there were only two keys—mine and the one I gave Mrs. Keate."

"And she's not a connoisseur?"

"I should hardly think so."

"All things considered, Miss Vance seems the likelier proposition. We have a good enough case to scare her with."

"Scare her into returning the picture?" Miss Paxton's eyes were brightening.

"There's a chance. People like Miss Vance hate the very thought of legal inquiries. They're bad for business, and judges and juries are not apt to be sympathetic with persons who make that kind of living."

Miss Paxton said after a pause: "I should never really take it into court, Henry; she's a member of the family, after all—Cousin Lawson's niece's only child; and she's young."

"I see the point; but we needn't tell Miss Vance so."

"If you really could frighten her into giving the picture back—"

Gamadge smiled. "The approach would have to be discreet, even devious. Would you mind that?"

"Not a bit!"

"She mustn't be put on her guard. Of course she'll always *be* on her guard, but perhaps I can work it so that she'll have to see me or practically admit she's afraid to. I may have to use your name."

"Do!"

"Let's go and telephone her now. You can hear exactly what I say, and what she says, and keep abreast of the whole thing."

"Henry Gamadge," said Miss Paxton, getting up, "you are the most satisfactory person I ever had dealings with."

"Thank you. Have you her address?"

"It's in the book; didn't I say?"

They went out into the hall again and back to the stair landing. Gamadge found the address in the book.

"Pretty far downtown," he said, "but on the east side." He dialed, and then held the receiver so that Miss Paxton could listen too.

After only a couple of rings a calm, rather high soprano voice said: "Yes?"

"I should like to speak to Miss Iris Vance, if you please. This is Henry Gamadge speaking, a friend of Miss Vance's relative Miss Julia Paxton."

There was a pause. Then the voice said: "This is Iris Vance."

"Oh—glad to find you at home, Miss Vance. I was calling on Miss Paxton today, and we were talking about the Ashbury family, and she mentioned the fact that you are a sensitive."

Another pause. Then Miss Vance said: "I did tell her so. I don't need or seek publicity."

"Miss Paxton mentioned the fact because I said I wanted to get into touch with someone who had extra-sensory gifts. A matter of clairvoyance, I think."

"Miss Paxton isn't sympathetic with that kind of thing; I am surprised that she should recommend me or anyone."

"It wasn't exactly a recommendation, Miss Vance. But if you care to call her up she'll give me one. I was very glad indeed to hear of somebody like you—one doesn't care to go into these matters entirely in the dark."

Ten seconds passed. Then Miss Vance said: "Might I ask what you wish to consult me about, Mr. Gamadge?"

Gamadge laughed. "You may as far as I'm concerned, but I have a rather skeptical friend whom I should like to convince in the matter. He's the kind who always talks about tests and watertight proof. As if such things followed mathematical formulas."

"Sometimes they almost do."

"I should like to be able to tell my friend that all tests have been complied with—that you knew nothing whatever in advance. I shouldn't even have told you my name if I'd thought you would be willing to see me without knowing it."

"I am rather careful about choosing my clients."

"Of course."

"Is the skeptical friend Miss Julia Paxton?"

"Now, Miss Vance, if you ask such questions as that the test will fail. Could you possibly see me this evening? The sooner the better, of course, from every point of view."

"From the skeptic's point of view, certainly. They think we have little black books and compare information, don't they?"

"I suppose so."

Miss Vance seemed to consider. Then she said: "Would ten o'clock be too late for you?"

"Not at all. Extremely kind of you to let me come."

"I'm going out to dinner, but I shall be at home before ten."

"Thank you so much."

Gamadge put down the receiver and turned to look at Miss Paxton with smug complacency. She returned his look with some consternation in her eye.

"Henry, you really are a most unscrupulous person."

"I tried to prepare you for that discovery."

"You're going to ask her to tell you what became of the other picture?"

"Something of the kind. As for my lack of scruples, do you think Miss Vance so scrupulous?"

"She can't help but suspect."

"And she simply must find out whether we do. If she refuses to see me, worse may befall than a private visit from someone who knows a member of the family. And she realizes that it may all be true—that I'm really a credulous ass who wants a clairvoyant. Have you any idea, Miss Paxton, how many otherwise hardheaded people in this city *do* want a clairvoyant? How many people more or less like us consult them all the time? Remember the Vances. You said they were cultivated and charming."

"But she may lose her temper and get you turned out."

"No violence," said Gamadge, following Miss Paxton back into her sitting room. "She wouldn't tackle the problem with violence. I'll take Lady Audley home with me, if you don't mind, frame and all. Those splinters under the nails are valuable evidence, and I want to look at them under a glass. I don't think they've had time to catch any dust at all, and the fresh wood under them is as clean as when it was new."

Miss Paxton fluttered about collecting paper and string. Gamadge wrote down his doctor's name and telephone number for her, picked up his hat and coat from the chair on which he had laid them when he came in, put the coat on, and took the wrapped picture under his arm. "Don't *you* see Miss Vance, you know," he instructed her. "And if she telephones, just repeat what I told her. You don't know a thing. You're in the hands of your agent now. Don't let her in. But how would you know who it was if the doorbell rang?"

"Look out first," said Miss Paxton, "or—I'll show you."

She caught up a golf cape—the last golf cape, Gamadge supposed, now existing in the Western world—and threw it over her shoulder. As he stood in the hall at the head of the stairs, she went along to the old front doors and opened one of them. She smiled at him over her shoulder. He laughed, nodded, went down and let himself out. Emerging from the portico, he looked up; she was standing on the little balcony, nodding and waving farewell.

A cab drove up, and Gamadge got into it. As they moved off downtown the driver commented on the pleasant scene they had left: "Cute old lady."

"Cute indeed."

As soon as he reached home—which was in the east Sixties—Gamadge went to his office. This was on the first floor, with a laboratory and darkroom behind it—a suite which had once been the Gamadge family's drawing room, dining room and pantry. The office retained its original molded ceiling and its fireplace, but was now lined with reference books and filing cabinets.

Gamadge unwrapped the aquatint, laid it on the broad desk between the windows, turned on a reading lamp, and hung his hat and coat on a chair. Harold Bantz, his former assistant, came out of the laboratory. He was staying with Gamadge while Mrs. Bantz and the little Bantz boy lodged with relatives in Connecticut. Harold was looking for an apartment.

Short, stocky, dark and morose of countenance, with a white blouse buttoned to his chin, he looked very much as he had looked ten years before when Gamadge took him, a destitute youth, off the street. But he was now a man of science.

He said: "I got those photographs of the Ranier forgeries developed."

"Thanks very much. Get the big reading glass, will you, and take a look at this?"

They examined the back of the picture, and signed a statement to the effect that the nails had been removed from the frame very recently. Then Gamadge turned the picture face up, and told Harold the story.

Harold said: "Funniest darn thing I ever heard of."

"Funny, yes." Gamadge looked at him inquiringly.

"Bad luck your dropping in on the old lady. I don't think she'd have done anything about it if you hadn't doped it out for her."

"No, I don't think so either. She didn't understand that there was any question of money involved, of course, and she's sensitive, as she naturally would be, to ridicule."

"Elderly people don't like it said they can't see straight."

"Or remember straight. She might have written to ask James Ashbury if he remembered lettering on the portrait, but she seemed to think he wouldn't know. I dare say he wouldn't. Now she's more than ever reluctant to mention it to him, because she wants to let the Vance girl off if she can."

"Let her off with a warning?"

"A scare."

"You think you can get a scare out of a professional medium?"

"If I spring the picture on her she might give herself away." Gamadge added: "What bothers you about it?"

"Mighty small profit for all that risk and trouble."

Gamadge was taking the portrait out of the frame. He said: "I know; but think of all the trouble some people take over a practical joke. Perhaps Miss Vance has a debased sense of humor."

"Couldn't be something bigger behind it?"

"Bigger?"

"Some racket. The house is made to order for it, the whole setup is. Plenty of things Miss Paxton wouldn't miss, plenty of stuff this James Ashbury doesn't know about at all. If Vance is mixed up in that kind of thing she could make a killing there. And if she's a medium and knows her business she already has a wax impression of Miss Paxton's latchkey."

Gamadge considered this doubtfully. "She could take the picture because she knew there was a duplicate in the house. What else could she take that Miss Paxton wouldn't miss?"

"I haven't seen what's there. But you could replace old glass and china—paperweights, ash trays, jade stuff—with plastics and junk from the five-and-ten. There's a market for everything now that was bought even fifty years ago, inflated values for gimcracks. And as for sales and the dealers, you hear a lot about people getting pleasant surprises when they dig out the old things in an old house; but they get unpleasant surprises a good deal oftener. You ought to know."

Gamadge was rolling the engraving up and wrapping it. He said: "Yes, I know. Everything's a museum piece to the heirs until they offer it to a museum."

"Here's something else: the old gentleman that owned the house—Lawson Ashbury. He lived alone there after his wife died?"

"So I gathered."

"If anybody got hold of his latchkey, they've had since last spring to do the looting; the house was standing empty."

"We can settle that."

"How?"

"There's burglary insurance." Gamadge sat down at the desk and pulled the telephone towards him. He dialed the Ashbury number. Miss Paxton answered. After a short and cheerful conversation with her he put the receiver down and turned to Harold. "There you are. The house was fully protected after Mr. Ashbury's death; wired with an alarm that rang at insurance headquarters. The agent had to cut off the alarm before he let Miss Paxton in. Nobody could open the door or any window without setting it off."

"O.K.," said Harold.

"And the small things James Ashbury picked out of the inventory—good stuff like Chinese curios and Battersea enamel—it was all there, and Miss Paxton says she remembered every piece of it."

"O.K., I'm licked."

CHAPTER FOUR

Séance

GAMADGE DID NOT know what was worn at séances, but he had an idea that upper spiritualistic circles were dressy. He therefore put on dinner clothes, and stood contemplating himself in a long mirror in the library when Harold came in for cocktails.

Harold said: "Don't break Vance's heart."

"Vance," replied Gamadge complacently, "will have to look after herself."

"I was just thinking: That picture's going to be a considerable shock for her. Don't mediums have bouncers to attend to scoffers that jolt them?"

"Miss Vance will placate me."

"Some day you're the one that's going to get the jolt."

"Let it come."

After dinner Gamadge wrote to his wife to tell her that he had deputized for her that afternoon. He wrote of the three thousand dollar income, and went on discreetly:

Miss Paxton had a nice little mystery waiting for me. I hope to solve it tonight. Harold takes it a little more seriously than I do, but as you know, he is always romantic. I think he misses that code he made up for us to use long ago before the war. Do you remember 'potto'? But of course he and I have used too many codes since then to find amusement in them now.

At twenty minutes to ten he stamped the letter and sallied forth into a crisp clear night, with a half moon riding high. He mailed the letter at the corner, and then came back and got into his car. He drove down Lexington, around Gramercy Park, and down Third almost to Fourteenth Street. He turned right, and stopped at a corner building on the south side of the street.

On the north side there were little brick houses, little dark shops; but Miss Vance's apartment house was the only residential structure on her block. Beyond it rose the blank walls of a storage warehouse, beyond that a factory. The street was deserted, and very dark.

The apartment house looked very old. Gamadge went up a short flight of steps into a vestibule, and through swing-doors into a high, dim, spacious lobby with a broad stairway at either end of it. The lobby was tiled and wainscoted, and had plaster walls of a sickly blue. There was no elevator.

The cubbyhole of an office on the left of the front door was empty, and contained no switchboard; but a list of names hanging just within the half-glass door told Gamadge that Miss Vance's flat was 5A.

With a groan, he began to climb the nearest stair. Under his arm he carried what looked like a roll of newspaper; it was in fact the evening paper, loosely wrapped about the rolled aquatint of Lady Audley.

In this generous old house there seemed to be only two apartments to a landing, with a door at either end of the wide hallways, and a door in the outer wall between that probably led to a fire exit. Gamadge, climbing on, reflected that when the place was built, elevators were only just coming in; people expected stairs. They also expected breathing space, elbow room, open fires, and plenty of people to carry coal scuttles and logs of wood. Balancing in his mind the pros and cons of the good old days, he reached the top story.

5A was just beyond the head of the stairway, with the fire door opposite the stair head. He traversed creaking floor boards and pushed the bell.

The door opened on a long, dark, narrow passage, beyond which there was a lighted room. Half hidden by the door, a young woman stood looking up at him; for the space of a few seconds they eyed each other silently. She saw a personable man with a stoop, carrying his evening paper in a rather slovenly roll under his arm; he saw a girl with a white skin, round hazel eyes, a mouth subtly curved. Her face was a rounded oval, framed in red hair that she wore to her shoulders. She looked faintly amused—more like a sprite, Gamadge thought, than a spirit.

She was wearing a long, brightly flowered green-and-yellow dress of some airy material, with floating sleeves. There were green sandals on her feet. She came out from behind the door and smiled. "Mr. Gamadge?"

"Miss Vance?"

"Yes, I'm Iris Vance. Will you leave your things on that chair, please? I'm sorry to say that my maid doesn't sleep in."

Gamadge laid his coat and hat on a chair. He retained the roll of newspapers, but Miss Vance had gone on to the lighted doorway beyond and did not seem to notice that he was bringing his bundle with him. He followed her into a large, bright, shabby room, with high studio windows, flowered rugs, wicker furniture, and vividly colored unframed pictures on the walls. Nothing, Gamadge thought, could be more unlike the popular idea of a witch's consulting room. Nothing could have surprised him much more than to see, when he looked towards the log fire, that four other persons were grouped about it. They were all looking at him.

"These clients had appointments for tonight too," said Miss Vance lightly, "and I didn't like to put them off—or to put you off. Do you really prefer a private sitting? A circle is always more effective."

"I don't in the least object to a circle," said Gamadge, "if you don't."

"Then may I introduce you?"

Gamadge stood looking urbanely at the other clients. They struck him as a very queer assortment, but perhaps in the circumstances a queer assortment was just what might be expected. Only...He had a sensitive perception to atmospheres, and he thought the group had at least one thing in common: a joke. The joke was on him. No—they had something else in common: a tenseness.

"Mrs. Spiker, Mr. Gamadge," said Miss Vance, standing beside him. Mrs. Spiker, who sat on the left of the fireplace with a half-filled glass in her hand, gave him a short nod. She was a large but shapely woman of perhaps forty, with lavishly applied coloring and bright blond hair. She wore big bright jewelry, a fashionable black dress, and a fantastic little spangled hat. Her shoes were hardly more than a crisscross of thin straps and a pair of very high heels.

"Miss Higgs," said Miss Vance.

Miss Higgs barely inclined her head. A very good-looking girl in her twenties, with an expression of languid disdain. She wore no hat, and her long velvet dress was rather informal. She might have been the product of a conventional bringing up and a fashionable school.

"Mr. Bowles," said Miss Vance.

Mr. Bowles was a little startling. He stood at the right-end side of the mantel, just behind Miss Higgs, and there was a glass on the shelf at his elbow. He was of medium height, dark, with heavy shoulders. He kept his heavy face lowered, and looked up at Gamadge from cold observant eyes. The eyes were a little sunken—Mr. Bowles might be needing sleep. He wore a blue pin-stripe suit that had not been pressed recently.

He muttered something that was meant to be affable.

The bouncer after all? thought Gamadge.

"And," said Miss Vance, "Mr. Simpson."

Mr. Simpson's suit had not been handed to him off a rack; nor did it need pressing. It was dark, well-cut and expensive. He was dark, well-made and expensive-looking himself. A young fellow, not more than twenty-five; brown-eyed, brown-haired, slim, self-confident. And if he's psychic, thought Gamadge, then so am I.

There was a big crystal globe on the mantel. Gamadge asked with naïve interest: "Do you use a globe, Miss Vance?"

"No, that's something I used to use. I don't use anything now. Won't you have a drink first, Mr. Gamadge? Before you tell us what you want to know?"

Mr. Simpson took a step towards a side table on which was a whiskey tray, but Gamadge shook his head. "No thanks, nothing for me. I won't keep you waiting. I'll get right down to business."

There was a long cherry-wood table below the windows, clear except for some big magazines. Gamadge went over to the table, heaped the magazines at one end of it, laid his parcel down, and unrolled it. Miss Vance came to stand beside him.

"Something has been lost," he said. "I thought this might help you to find it."

"By clairvoyance?"

"By clairvoyance of course."

"Sometimes a related object does help."

"This is a related object." Gamadge stripped off the inside wrapping of brown paper, and laid the aquatint face upwards on the table. He kept it flat with both hands, and looked at Iris Vance. She stood absolutely still. Wonderful control of the muscles, Gamadge thought.

The group by the fire watched her. Moments passed.

"I see that you remember Lady Audley," said Gamadge. "You would, naturally."

She slowly raised her eyes and looked at Gamadge with polite inquiry. "Know it? To my knowledge I've never seen it before."

"I'm sorry to hear that; I thought you'd remember it, since it comes from the Ashbury house on Park Avenue."

"I haven't been there, except for a short call on Miss Paxton last Sunday afternoon, for many years. Not since I was a child."

"So she told me."

"What has been lost, Mr. Gamadge?"

"The other Lady Audley, a much better one; what is called a proof before letter. You know what that is?"

"No, I really don't."

"An engraving with no inscription on it. It hung in the hall until—let me see—Sunday evening. Then it developed letters—all this..." Gamadge ran his finger along the lettering. "Miss Paxton noticed that it had done so, and mentioned the queer fact to me today."

She looked down at the picture, and then up at him again. "I really don't understand at all."

"You've never met another such case of this kind of spirit writing?"

"I never even heard of such a thing."

"I'm so ignorant about the occult. I hoped you could explain it. A proof before letter is so much more valuable, you know."

Mr. Bowles asked loudly: "How much more valuable?"

"Fifty to seventy dollars difference. Rather a mischievous kind of trick for a spirit to play," said Gamadge. "Malicious, I call it."

Miss Higgs spoke in a low, rather husky voice: "Let's see the thing."

Gamadge held it up by its top and bottom edges. "Nice thing," he said. "Supposed to resemble Miss Vance's great-uncle's mother. Miss Paxton knew it well; that's why she noticed that lettering had sprouted out on it. She's worried—feels responsible."

Mr. Simpson said after a silence: "I thought something was supposed to be lost."

"Well, that's of course the alternative," Gamadge told him. "That the pictures were changed. This one was in the house in a kind of book-room— I mean it may have been. At any rate, the other is gone—either really gone, or supernaturally changed into what you see. If Miss Vance could tell us by clairvoyance what has happened to it, well, I needn't say what a relief that would be to poor Miss Paxton." He laid the portrait down again and turned to face Miss Vance. "Or if you can't help her in that way, she thought it was just possible that you might be able to suggest some dealer who would be able to replace the other portrait. She tells me that your father was an artist, perhaps you have some knowledge of this sort. The thing wouldn't be so easy to find. Miss Paxton wondered if you could possibly be persuaded to hunt one up among the galleries. Anything to get it back, you know, without a fuss and complications."

Simpson had stepped a little forward, but nobody spoke. Then Miss Vance laughed gaily, threw out her arms so that the sleeves floated like wings, and let her hands fall. She said: "This is stupid. He's laughing at us."

Miss Higgs was scowling. Bowles was shaking his head at Mr. Simpson, but the young man walked up to Gamadge and spoke furiously: "What do you mean by all this? What's the idea?"

Iris Vance replied, still gaily, "He thinks I'm an underworld character. He thinks I stole the thing. No, really, when you come to think of it, what a joke on me!"

Bowles came forward, a man who seemed to lumber but was light on his feet. He said: "Wait a minute, wait a minute," and went up to the table. He leaned over the engraving, frowned at it, bent to read the lettering. Then he swung on Gamadge. "Let's hear some more about this. Where was the other one hanging in that house?"

"Towards the rear of the first-floor hall."

"Framed?"

"Framed."

"And we're to take your word for it that the frame could have been tampered with?"

"And Miss Paxton's word for it. My opinion is that it had been tampered with, and recently."

"Then all this stuff about spirit writing was phony? You didn't mean it? You didn't even expect Miss Vance to fall for it?"

"It was an approach. It wasn't I, you know, who let in anybody else on our sitting. Miss Vance was free to respond as she chose."

"Well, of all the—"

Mrs. Spiker now spoke, roughly but with a kind of careless good humor: "Don't waste any of that on this guy, he's too slick. Iris, go ahead and tell him you don't have to go around picking up fifty dollars that way." Simpson was about to speak, but she cut in on him: "No, it's her business."

"Yes," said Miss Higgs shortly. "It certainly is."

"And I could have told you he didn't believe in spirits," added Mrs. Spiker, "one minute after he came into this room. Look at him."

"I'm looking at him." Bowles lowered at Gamadge. "He's out to get some picture back, he thinks he has proof Miss Vance has it, and he'll hang on to his idea whatever she says."

Mr. Simpson's face was a study in frustration. He walked over to the side table and poured himself a drink.

"That's right," said Miss Vance, her eyes following him. "That's what we all need." She looked at Gamadge, and he thought there was an anxious expression in her round eyes. "It's all a mistake, you know, Mr. Gamadge. Some mistake of Miss Paxton's. I thought when I was there that she was a very old lady to be doing all that work and sorting out all those things. Of course she forgets, and mixes things up. There are dozens of pictures in that hall—I remember that much about it."

Miss Higgs was now supplied with a highball; she thanked Mr. Simpson, crossed one leg over the other, drank, and then spoke coolly:

"My advice is to go and find a picture. Tell Miss Paxton you're going to find a picture, and go out and find one. I don't think it would do any good to offer her the fifty or seventy dollars, or whatever it is; just go and get a picture for her and take it up there."

Simpson stood glaring at her. "And how does Iris find the picture?" he asked.

Miss Higgs shrugged her shoulders.

Simpson clenched his hands. "J—j—just keep out of this," he said between his teeth.

Miss Vance walked up to him and put her hand on his arm. "It's all my fault, Jim. Let me just explain to Mr. Gamadge, and it will be all right. Pull up a chair for him, and we'll all sit down and have highballs and talk it over. He'll understand."

"He'll understand about you," said Bowles, whose lower lip was protruding as he again studied the calm face of Lady Audley. "But what about this?"

"Miss Paxton made a mistake. The picture always had that lettering on it, that's all."

"And that's enough." Mrs. Spiker put out one of her silk-clad legs and touched the rung of the chair next to her with a silk-clad toe. "Sit down, Mr. Who. Have a drink and listen to the kid. You look to me like a sensible man. You had your fun, you can't prove a thing, now you'll find out that she wouldn't any more take somebody else's stuff than she'd jump out of the window. She don't have to. She'd be crazy to."

Simpson had pushed up another chair. Iris Vance sat down, Gamadge sat down. He again refused whiskey, but accepted a light for his cigarette from the obliging Mrs. Spiker.

"That's right," she said, "don't drink with strangers. You'll change your mind later. I hope so, anyway, because you're the kind of feller I like. Go right after what you want. What's this Miss Paxton to you, by the way?"

"Old friend of my wife's, and a nice old lady. I don't care to see her victimized."

"She hasn't been."

Bowles had gone back to his position at the end of the chimney piece, Simpson sat down behind Iris Vance. She turned to Gamadge:

"It was just my idiotic idea of a joke, Mr. Gamadge—to tell Miss Paxton that I was a medium, and to keep it up afterwards when you telephoned. I'm not a medium. I never was one professionally—for money—and I haven't even pretended to be one since I was fifteen years old. I'm a commercial artist."

"This is a surprise," said Gamadge.

"I used to pretend to be a medium when I was a child," said Miss Vance, "but I never believed in it, and I had no powers at all."

"And whatever you do," said Mrs. Spiker, looking truculently at Gamadge, "don't act shocked about it. The kid wasn't to blame."

"I'm not acting shocked," said Gamadge mildly.

CHAPTER FIVE

Warning

MISS VANCE SAID: "You will be shocked, of course. And I don't know who was to blame if I wasn't."

Simpson muttered: "You won't let anybody blame your father and mother."

"They believed in something and brought me up to believe in it. That's all they did. The rest was entirely my own idea." She turned her head to look at Gamadge. "They were wonderful people, Mr. Gamadge. Utterly unworldly. But thanks to my father I can make a living at so-called art."

"Are those yours?" Gamadge raised his eyes to a flower piece over the mantel, and looked at others to the right and left of it. "They're charming."

"But you can see how I've missed the real thing. My excuse is that I had my living to earn, and now I do more than that; but—the dyer's hand, you know. Everything I do looks like something that ought to have a slogan under it. 'The perfume of these roses has not the *effect* of Lancelot's Rose Witchery.'"

Mrs. Spiker burst out laughing. "You ought to do the copy too."

Miss Vance gave her an elvish smile. "And who says I don't? But Mr. Gamadge isn't interested in all this. He can check up on me and find out that I'm not likely to risk my reputation and my income for the sake of fifty dollars. Even a kleptomaniac wouldn't, and I don't think kleptomania comes into it. They don't take things like pictures, do they? They like bright things."

Bowles said: "Take anything, but if you ask me there isn't much kleptomania in the world. That's a fancy name for good old plain thieving."

Simpson said angrily: "It's nothing a kleptomaniac would take—a framed engraving off a wall. Don't waste time on it. Just make this Mr. Gamadge understand that you don't need small sums of money."

"I understand," said Gamadge.

"But you don't understand why I let you think I was a medium," said Iris Vance.

"Or why you let Miss Paxton think so. For the matter of that, I don't know why you let Mr. Lawson Ashbury go on thinking so."

"And let myself be cut out of his will? Oh, but he would never have put me in his will, not if I'd gone down on my knees to him. I'll have to tell you the whole story. It's a funny story, Mr. Gamadge; it's one of the funniest stories you ever heard in your life."

Simpson, who sat leaning forward with his hands clasped, looking at the floor, remarked that it wasn't such a funny story.

"The poor kid," remarked Mrs. Spiker, who seemed much more at ease than the rest of the party, "was brought up on spooks from the day she was born. And what she did, she did to please the folks."

Gamadge was watching Miss Higgs. She sat with her shoulder turned to Gamadge, her eyes on the fire. Detached and silent, she seemed to have excluded herself from the group and from the conversation.

"I was a wretchedly precocious child," said Iris Vance. "I was deceitful. I still am. I thought it would be such fun to let you come here and have a séance—make a fool of you. My friends— when they dropped in I told them about the joke, and they rather reluctantly agreed to sit in on it. Put on a show with all the trimmings. If I'd known why you were coming—but that's no use. As for Miss Paxton, well, she *is* a nice old lady, but when I came on Sunday she evidently had such a horror of me—from what she'd been told by the Ashburys—that I couldn't resist playing up. The Ashburys were stuffy, you know, very stuffy. If I'd told Uncle Lawson the whole truth he would have thought it much worse than what he'd thought about me before.

"Well, I've had my second warning. I won't tempt the spirits again."

"Warning?" asked Gamadge.

"You'll hear. As for this one, I quite see it. If Miss Paxton hadn't thought I was a professional cheat she never would have suspected me of stealing a picture, and neither would you. I should just have been a nice hard-working young commercial artist, making a Sunday call on a distant relative—by invitation."

"Pretty quick thinking," said Simpson ironically, "for you to dope out the whole picture business that afternoon."

"But they'll tell you," Miss Vance smiled at him, "that mediums have to be quick thinkers. They do. I'm out of practice now," she went on to Gamadge, "I stopped ten years ago. But I began young; I couldn't have been more than seven or eight when I produced my first effect at home for my parents' benefit. A modest effect, but I'd seen what the professionals did, and I was clever. I did it as a kind of game."

"They took you to séances—at that age?" asked Gamadge wonderingly.

"You don't understand—it was their religion; it was all beautiful to them."

"But what could you do—at that age?"

"If you'll read up on spiritualism, Mr. Gamadge"—she smiled at him—"you'll find that where there are poltergeists there are often children—sometimes young children. And you must remember that my parents wouldn't question the validity of the phenomena—they wouldn't question me. They weren't psychics—they couldn't produce effects, and they would have died rather than pretend to. They never dreamed that I'd pretend to. And I—well, I never explained that it wasn't the spirits, it was only me."

"Kids like to be important," said Mrs. Spiker.

"I can only say that I went on producing phenomena, better and better ones. My father and mother wanted to be deluded, but before long I could delude almost anybody. We never made a penny out of it, of course, but I was taken about and shown off to believers."

"Bad medicine for a kid," remarked Bowles, and drained his glass. He went to the side table and refilled it.

"Well, in a way it made very little impression on me," said Iris Vance. "You must remember that I was a skeptic from the first, and that on the whole I had a normal life. I went to school, I played with other children, and my father was teaching me to draw and paint.

"By the time I was ten, I had developed a technique in other things than art. I practised regularly. I had my own methods. Once I performed in the presence of a very well-known professional, in broad daylight. I shall never forget the expression on her face as she watched me—she was on! Afterwards she got me into a corner; a big, rather frightening woman she was, with a great European renown. She said: 'My leetle wan, remember this: remember it the first time they catch you. It will not matter to you to be caught, because it will not matter to those who matter to *you*.'

"She got caught, and she went to jail. But she came out, and she went right on with her profession. Never lost a client."

Bowles came back to his place, and put his glass down on the mantel shelf. "Big money in it," he said.

"If you materialize. But that's risky."

Gamadge said: "The faithful always understand that when inspiration fails, the medium hates to let the audience down."

"Yes," said Iris Vance. "The one thing they can't face is to lose faith themselves."

"Did the Ashburys catch you?"

"Certainly not!" She assumed a look of deep offense. "The Ashburys! I'd better tell you about that. We paid that fatal call, and I must explain that we were only tolerated on the understanding that spiritualism must never be mentioned. My father and mother amiably conformed to that prejudice. They'd never dared to say that I was gifted. They'd told me not to talk about my gift to Great-uncle Lawson and Great-aunt Marietta, but as usual I was too clever for my own good, and so swollen by vanity that I thought a demonstration would bring Uncle and Aunt shouting into the fold. I'd brought my favorite tackle along with me, my reel of shoe-thread, weighted at one end with a padded dress weight; in case you never saw one, they're little perforated discs made of lead. I found mine in my mother's old workbox.

"The drawing room was crowded with furniture and bric-a-brac. Aunt and Uncle and my father and mother sat in a circle in front of the gas fire. After tea I was allowed to wander about behind them, looking at things. I never broke anything.

"Great-uncle was in one of those high-backed upholstered chairs, and I can see the yellow satin now and feel it. I stood behind it with my left hand on the round back."

"I think," said Gamadge, "that I saw it this afternoon."

"Did you see a little table, a sort of étagére on wheels? It used to stand between the windows, laden with knickknacks."

"No, I didn't see it."

"Well, I saw it; and I saw that it was standing on a six-foot space of bare hardwood floor. I couldn't resist—it was too much for me. Something"—she smiled—"got into me. Anyway, I took my little lariat out of my pocket, got it ready—all with one hand, I never took the other off the back of the chair—and swung it. The weighted end coiled round a leg of the little table on wheels, and I pulled. The table came rolling along as if it had the devil in it."

Mrs. Spiker burst into her loud laugh. "Wish I'd been there."

"Oh, it was awful. Uncle saw it first, got half up, and choked out something. Aunt Marietta looked round and gave a scream. I rushed forward, put both hands on the table—of course it began to rock like mad—and called out: 'It came right to me!' Things fell off it, and I got down and began to pick them up—and to uncoil my weight, and reel up my black thread.

"Aunt Marietta fainted. She was in bed for a week. We never entered the house again.

"And my poor parents were prouder of me than ever, though they had great expectations from the Ashburys, and we were quite poor."

There was a silence. Then Miss Vance asked in a matter-of-fact tone: "Well, Mr. Gamadge, do you think the Lawson Ashburys or Miss Paxton would have liked this version better than the other one?"

"I'm afraid not. That was your first warning, Miss Vance, to leave the spirits alone?"

"Oh, no! I practised for five years more, until I was fifteen. When my first warning came I was as much frightened as poor Great-aunt Marietta had been."

Miss Higgs slowly turned her head and looked at Iris Vance. She said: "I never heard of that."

"No, I don't talk about it, but this seems to be an occasion for frankness. I was so frightened that I never pretended to be a medium again, I never even went to a séance. I think my parents explained it by some quirk of adolescence—my losing my gift. They were grieved when I lost it—and my interest—but they didn't reproach me or argue. They never did."

Mrs. Spiker asked: "For Heaven's sake what happened?"

"You may not think much of it. It was at a dark séance that some friends of ours had requested, and there were a good many people there. I was in a trance, and my control was talking. I had a control, of course, by that time, a very nice sympathetic one named Ozima. She had a slight foreign accent, which of course was understandable, since she was an ancient Aztec. She talked as I should talk if I had a slight cold in my head and a gumdrop in both cheeks."

Simpson moved his feet and coughed.

"Not very nice, is it?" She smiled at him. "Not very nice for the real spirits—if there should happen to be any. At any rate, I felt a tap on my shoulder."

"What?" Miss Higgs stared at her.

"Something or somebody tapped me hard on the shoulder. A call to order—that's what it felt like. Well, I suppose I must have been a neurotic child after all; it had a frightful effect on me."

Bowles said after a moment: "Somebody playing a joke on *you*, for a change."

"Perhaps. Whoever it was moved very quietly and fast."

"Somebody smuggled a skeptic in."

"I hoped so. I'd often heard or read of skeptics who once—just once—while they were investigating frauds, you know, happened on something they couldn't explain. I was a skeptic, and I know what they meant...Or was I a skeptic after all? I wonder."

Gamadge said: "I always thought it only meant that for once the investigator ran up against somebody that was too clever even for him."

"I thought of that. But it's different when it happens."

Mrs. Spiker said loudly: "The whole business had you a nervous wreck. It was a crime. Fifteen years old—heading for a crash."

Miss Vance looked up at the crystal globe on the mantel. "I've pretended to see things in that globe many times. I keep it as a reminder not to look again. I haven't. Tonight I thought it would be a good joke to pretend to, but Mr. Gamadge tapped me on the shoulder."

"Well," said Gamadge, "I'm flesh and blood anyhow."

"You take the whole thing too seriously," said Mr. Simpson. "Forget it. Doesn't amount to anything. I don't know why you told that story, Iris. Damned if I know."

Miss Higgs smiled. "I know. Iris told the story, the whole story, because she thinks Mr. Gamadge may be persuaded to believe that that thing"—she nodded towards the engraving that lay, with its top and bottom edges curled, on the far table—"really is haunted."

There was a curious pause. Nobody protested, and she went on: "She thinks that will settle it. She thinks he'll go back and tell Miss Paxton that it's the original picture, treated by ghosts; or that the original picture had that inscription on it, faded out, and then for some occult reason changed back again. That is, of course, if he believed the story."

"I believe every word of it," said Gamadge.

"So do I. But it won't make you think that the spirits brought out writing on the picture." She glanced at Iris, a curious glance. "Have you no sense of character? He'll keep at it and keep at it, unless you simply tell him you did take the picture, and that you'll give it back."

Simpson shouted at her: "How do you think she's going to give it back when she never had it? You don't find the things growing on bushes, Gamadge said so himself."

"You know I never took it," said Iris.

"Well, then." Miss Higgs shrugged and turned her face towards the fire once more.

Again that curious pause, as if they were all holding their breath. Gamadge rose and glanced from face to face; not one of them was looking at him.

He went over to the table, rolled the aquatint in the brown paper, left the newspapers, and crossed to the door. Miss Vance was there before him. She stood silent while he put on his coat.

"Well," he said, looking down at her gravely, "I'm very sorry I can't subscribe to the ghost theory. Did you really expect me to?"

"I hoped you would."

"Less bother, of course. Miss Paxton couldn't very well put it in the inventory, though, could she?"

"Do you still think I'd steal a picture?"

"Certainly not for the value of it in money. I don't know what to think, and that's a fact."

"Then can't you drop the whole thing? Miss Paxton would if you advised her to."

"I'm acting for her, Miss Vance. How can I drop it?"

She made a resigned gesture with both hands. "It's all my fault. I made a bad impression on you. If I hadn't been a fool I'd have seen you alone."

Gamadge smiled and shook his head. She opened the outer door, and he went out and down the stairs.

CHAPTER SIX

Escape For One

THE STAIRS WERE slippery old waxed stairs that had never been carpeted; Gamadge went down them carefully, his parcel under his right arm and his left hand on the rail. He asked himself questions to which he could find no answer.

These friends that had dropped in on Miss Iris Vance were an ill-assorted group, but they seemed to know one another well and to have an understanding. What were two toughs like Mrs. Spiker and Mr. Bowles doing in a circle that included Miss Higgs and Mr. Simpson? Miss Vance might have acquaintances in two worlds, but how had she managed to bring them together in amity?

Miss Higgs and Mr. Simpson were not toughs in the same sense that Mr. Bowles and Mrs. Spiker were toughs, but in their own way they were cool propositions; knew their way about, young as they were. Nothing soft or meek about Miss Higgs and Mr. Simpson, and Miss Higgs really seemed to think that Iris Vance had stolen the Audley portrait. Yet how meek, comparatively speaking, they had all been—even Mrs. Spiker. They had repressed themselves. Simpson was in love with Miss Vance, so far as Gamadge could tell, but his interference had been almost perfunctory, and the tough Bowles had quelled it. What were they afraid of?

Gamadge thought that they were afraid of something apart from the discovery that the picture had been changed; he was almost sure that none of them except Miss Vance had ever heard of the picture before that evening. What had worried them about it was simply that it was making trouble.

They couldn't afford trouble. Well, people who went about under false names seldom could afford it. Gamadge was reasonably certain that Miss Vance had introduced all of her friends to him by false names.

He had reached the middle of the next flight when he came to this conclusion, but at that point his thoughts were interrupted. A roar and a crash seemed to echo all around him. Startled out of his wits, he lost his footing; his feet flew out in front of him, and he came down on the edge of a step with a jar that all but dislocated his spine. The picture shot from under his arm, bounded all the way to the landing below, and unrolled itself. His dazed eye caught Lady Audley's, and to his shattered imagination she seemed to gaze at him with even more than her usual reserve.

He was dimly aware that something had hit the wainscot a little above and behind him. He turned his head, and at sight of a small splintered hole in the woodwork struggled to his feet. Harold dashed along the landing below, rounded the turn of the stair rail, and came to a stop, breathing hard. His Colt automatic was in his hand.

He asked: "Are you shot?"

"By you?" Gamadge, a hand pressed to his injured vertebrae, glared at him.

"Me? How would I hit you?"

"I don't know." Gamadge turned again to look at the hole in the woodwork.

"That wasn't me," said Harold. "I was shooting straight up from the lower hall. This place is built like a birdcage; you can see straight up to the top floor."

Gamadge was still confused; he stood rubbing his spine and staring.

The door of the apartment at that end of the lower landing opened, and an old gentleman looked out into the hall, and then at the two on the stairs above him. Harold's pistol was now not in evidence.

The old gentleman came out. He wore an ancient claret-colored smoking jacket, and he had a pipe in his hand. He asked: "What was that noise?"

Harold said: "My friend fell downstairs."

The old gentleman looked at Gamadge. "Injured?"

"Not permanently, I think."

"I should have said that ten people fell downstairs." Mildly disgusted, the old gentleman went back into his flat and shut the door. Harold dashed up to the top floor, but returned immediately. He said: "Nobody around. What's been going on?"

"You tell me."

"Tell you why anybody wanted to shoot you?"

"Tell me why you fired off that forty-five of yours and scared the life out of me."

"If I hadn't you wouldn't be alive. I was standing down there waiting for you, wondering if it was you coming down, and I saw a hand with a gun in it come over the top-floor rail. There's only one way to stop a shot—shoot first. I shot straight up, and I guess the party's gun went off out of nervousness. That"—he nodded at the hole in the wainscot—"is about where it would land."

Gamadge repeated: "Hand with a gun in it?"

"Listen, you fell down; O.K. Didn't hit your head, did you?"

Gamadge shook it.

"Then get thinking. I said a hand with a gun in it. Hand in a dark coat-sleeve, and that's all I saw, and I was pretty good to see that, four flights up in a dim light."

"That's why the noise seemed to come from everywhere; two guns."

"That's right." Harold nodded approvingly. "You're getting it now. Keep at it. Two guns. One was aimed at you, short range and no fooling. Mine scared the party off—party didn't know somebody was covering you."

"How did you happen to be down there?"

"I didn't like the sound of the setup. You brushed me off."

Gamadge suddenly regained his faculties. He said: "Here, give me that," snatched the .45 from Harold's hand, stuffed it into his coat pocket, and ran up the stairs to the top floor. He put his finger on Miss Vance's bell and kept it there.

She opened the door at once. She looked very white and shaken; she was wearing a dark tweed coat, and she held a stamped addressed letter in her hand.

Gamadge asked: "Hear the row?"

"Row?"

"I fell downstairs."

"Oh, I'm so—the elevated trains make such a noise when they go by. I never hear anything. I'm so sorry."

They were both speaking almost absently; as if their minds were elsewhere, and there was no sense in concealing the fact.

Gamadge said: "Excuse me for bothering you, but I think I left my cigarette case."

"Oh, did you?"

It was the timeworn excuse that didn't matter. Gamadge went past her into the living room, which was now lighted by only one shaded lamp. Miss Higgs, Mr. Simpson, Mrs. Spiker and Mr. Bowles had disappeared.

Gamadge asked shortly: "What's become of the gang? Did they dematerialize, or leave by the fire stairs?"

"They went to Miss Higgs' apartment down the hall."

"Five B?"

"Yes. She lives there."

"Funny. I didn't see 'Higgs' on the manager's list in the office."

"It's a sublet."

"Oh. These are nice flats—mind if I look over yours, now I'm here?"

Again without apology, he walked down an inner passage; past a small dining room, a bedroom, a kitchen. At the end of the passage there was a bath. Nobody anywhere. He came back.

"Very nice," he said. "I'm being rude, but it's such a shock to fall downstairs. Well, good night again, and thanks for putting in a good word for me—I suppose you did?"

She looked at him blankly.

"But it didn't do any good. Well, I've been lucky. Let me mail your letter for you."

She yielded it up without a word. He passed her, went along the front hall to the door, let himself out, and closed the door behind him.

Harold was where Gamadge had left him, digging at the hole in the woodwork with his pocketknife. He held up a bullet. "It's a little one. Did you get the gun it came out of?"

"I wasn't fool enough to try." Gamadge went on down to the foot of the stairs, picked up the aquatint, and rolled it, "Come on."

Harold followed him. "What did you go up there for, then? I thought you were going to stand them all up with my pistol."

"What for? The gun you saw probably left the building some time ago by way of the fire stairs. There must be an alley to Third Avenue. Miss Vance had four friends with her—she says they're now in Five B. Why tackle them? I couldn't establish identities, that's for the police. I couldn't do much with one gun against perhaps three. I went back principally to show Miss Vance that I was alive."

"You have a right to be dead twice over—going up there to that flat alone."

"They wouldn't shoot me in her flat. They could have shot me before if they'd been willing to do it up there. But a casualty on the stairs that's different. Plenty of robberies with violence now, people sneaking into apartment buildings and committing murder; and there's always the fire exit. But I'd better tell you the story, so that you'll know what I'm talking about."

As they left the building, Harold remarked that everybody in it, including the superintendent, seemed to be at the movies or sound asleep, except the old gentleman who thought two guns going off—one of them a forty-five calibre Colt automatic—sounded like people falling downstairs.

"The flats have long passageways to the living rooms, and an inside hall. And as Miss Vance reminded me, the elevated runs past the East end of the house."

They got into the car, and Gamadge started it. He said: "By the way, I haven't expressed my gratitude."

"Never mind it," replied Harold with dignity. "I wouldn't want you to get mushy about it."

"I was preoccupied. Thanks for my life. I still don't know why you thought it necessary to come. These people don't make much sense to me."

"Or to me. I wanted to mention that. But after you left I kept thinking that these mediums have tough friends, and they don't like a showdown, and the whole business seemed bigger to me than it did to you."

"It is bigger. Miss Vance says she isn't a medium."

"No?"

"Hasn't even pretended to supernatural powers for ten years. I'm inclined to believe her."

"She has tough friends, though."

"Evidently. Two, at least." Gamadge described the party in detail.

When he had finished, Harold said: "You certainly busted in on something. You say the Vance girl had a dark-brown coat on when you went back to the flat. Probably on her way out to see whether you were really killed or not. Don't think too much about that friendly warning she gave you, you only imagined she meant to warn you. Where's that letter she said she was going to mail?"

Gamadge fished it out of his pocket. Harold looked at it. It was addressed to a well-known advertising company.

"Fits in with the commercial art job," he said. "I'm glad something fits in." He added, as the car swung around a corner, "Hey, why are you going to Park?"

"You don't suppose I'd leave Miss Paxton in a thing like this if there's shooting in it? She's getting out of that house tonight if I have to pack for her myself. If she won't move, I'll stay there till she does."

"But it wouldn't make *any* sense for them to get after her now; you got away. Their gunman knew that, anyhow."

"It wouldn't make sense, but I don't understand how their minds work; neither, from what you said a while ago, do you. There isn't a chance in a thousand that she's in any danger, but I won't take even part of a chance."

"With you loose they'd never touch her in the world. You'd establish a connection with Vance. They couldn't risk it."

"For some reason they risked having a shot at me."

"Yes, and if they'd got you Miss Paxton would have set the police on them. And if they got you both they'd still be risking their necks on the chance that you hadn't said anything about the case to anybody else. Some risk. You'd talked to me."

"And I wrote to Clara. I didn't say much, but I said enough."

"Perhaps they're all so dog-goned stupid they think there isn't enough connection. Miss Paxton tells you something about a picture that can't be proved, you come to see Miss Vance about it, and a robber shoots at you in the outside hall."

"They're not stupid."

"It certainly looks as though you never had a dog's chance—if I hadn't happened to show up—of getting out of the place alive tonight. The sequence of events—not a hitch in it. You telephone Vance, making an appointment; you've mentioned Miss Paxton to her, and that's enough—the whole gang has to sit in on it and hear what you have to say. Vance puts the hour late, so that they can all be there.

"When you get there they're all under a strain. You produce the picture—"

"Slight hitch at that point," said Gamadge. "None of them except Miss Vance seemed to know anything about it, and Miss Higgs seemed to think Miss Vance did steal it. And she didn't care who knew that she thought so."

"Never mind, you're making trouble for Miss Vance and sticking to it that something's wrong. You've brought the Ashbury house into it. You're dead. Vance told you that ghost story to keep you there late. What time was it when you didn't get shot?"

"Just after eleven."

"Halls apt to be clear, people home and settling down. It's all there," said Harold, "and it doesn't add up to a thing."

"And just to make it harder, I think they were all introduced to me by false names."

"False names?"

"They all seemed to know one another pretty well, but they never used a name—a Christian name—except Iris Vance's, and except when she made one slip and called Mr. Simpson Jim. He nearly made a slip too; he began to call Miss Higgs something that also began with a J, but he stammered over it and said something else. He never stammered again."

"Their real names would have given you some warning, then."

"If they can't face inquiry they've all left by this time, Miss Higgs and all."

The car had entered the dark and quiet upper reaches of Park Avenue. Harold said: "You might have telephoned Miss Paxton."

"I could never have got her out of the house by telephone, and perhaps she wouldn't have heard the telephone. She may be asleep, and the telephone is on the floor below her bedroom."

"Why will she hear the doorbell, then?"

"If she doesn't, I'll stay there and you can get cops." He added: "One thing—she'd never let anybody in at this time of night without mighty careful scouting."

"And they didn't get much of a start. And they wouldn't care to make much of a fuss trying to get in. I'm inclined to think," said Harold, "that your terrible experience on the staircase shook up your brains a little."

"Perhaps so. I don't like it when people who are not crazy act as if they were."

They had reached the Ashbury block. Gamadge drove to the upper corner, rounded the island, and came down on the West side of the street. He got out of the car, and then stood still. He was facing a uniformed policeman who looked at him from the dark of the portico.

After a moment Gamadge asked: "Something wrong here?"

"Accident."

"Accident? What kind of—I know the lady in this house."

"Fatal accident." The policeman jerked his head upwards. Gamadge lifted his eyes and saw that the iron railing in front of the old doorway was askew, and that one of the doors was open. Another policeman came out on the ledge, tugged the rail straighter, went back into the house, and shut the door behind him with a boom.

"What in God's name happened?" asked Gamadge.

"She fell out."

"Fell out!"

"That's right."

"When?" Gamadge's tone was so harsh and peremptory that the policeman took offense at it. He said: "Read it in the morning papers."

Gamadge spoke more quietly: "Just tell me when."

"The body was found about a quarter past nine. It couldn't have laid out here long without being seen."

"Thanks."

Gamadge turned and walked back to the car. Harold had been hanging out of the window; he withdrew his head as Gamadge walked around the car and got in.

The car started with what seemed like a leap. Harold said: "Watch it. No use getting pinched." He sat with his eyes fixed on Gamadge's profile. After a minute he said: "She was dead an hour before you ever got to the Vance apartment house."

"Yes."

"Where are we going?"

"Precinct. They'll have what information there is."

Harold said after another pause: "I suppose Vance had to let you come tonight—take a chance on it. If she hadn't let you come you might have tried to get in touch with Miss Paxton."

"Whatever happened, this changes everything."

CHAPTER SEVEN

Peculiar Accident

"**I**T WAS A PECULIAR ACCIDENT," said Detective-Lieutenant Nordhall, "but I think they got it all doped out, how and why it happened."

He and Gamadge sat in a little office, facing each other across the scarred top of a desk. Gamadge was leaning back in his hard chair, his eyes closed, his legs stretched out, his feet crossed, his hands clasped on his waistline. Nordhall had papers before him.

"The boys here would have given you all the details," continued Nordhall. "I don't know why you dragged me out. But I understand you're interested, want to tell your wife all about it. Sorry this Miss Paxton was a friend of her folks.

"Well, here's everything, and probably a little more than you expected; when there's a fatality like this we make a point of notifying the family. We don't wait till they read it in the paper.

"The reason the accident was peculiar is because the house is peculiar, as you know. Old Mr. Lawson Ashbury—

well-known business character in New York, wholesale cotton goods—he was quite sore when the city made him take off his front stoop. Said he wasn't going to put a lot of money into remodeling a house that might get blasted out from under him the next time some improvement fanatic took a whim. So he did the job the way you saw, and a lot of other house-holders did the same. Economy with some of them, not with Mr. Lawson Ashbury. He was very well fixed.

"We got this dope from his son James Ashbury of San Francisco, the Department called him up long distance at a little after ten o'clock." Nordhall took a small red leather notebook out of an envelope. "This is Miss Paxton's address book; that's how the Department got James Ashbury's address. The old lady's handbag was on her sitting-room table, the only lighted room in the house at the time of the accident; had her identification card in it, Tarrytown address and telephone numbers, everything. We called up some Tarrytown people too."

Gamadge had half opened his eyes to look at the address book. Now he felt for a cigarette.

"Ashbury was upset," continued Nordhall. "Seems a very nice kind of feller, and free with his money. He don't want to come East, no reason why he should, and he's given us carte blanche for all expenses. Wiring us money, in fact.

"Mr. Ashbury and the Department got it all straightened out, what happened to the poor old lady tonight. Ashbury wrote and asked her to go to the house and stay there while the agents were selling off and closing up—you know that. She decided to do most of the work herself, see purchasers and dealers and so on. Wrote him that the change and the visit to New York would be a treat for her. But you know all that. Ashbury hardly remembers her, but he knew she knew the house well—used to stay there with his parents in the old days—and he thought she'd be an ideal person for the job if she wasn't too old for it. She wrote him she wasn't. How did she strike you?"

Gamadge had not lighted his cigarette. He held it in his fingers, slowly rolling it between them. "Not too old," he said.

"Ashbury thought so too, from the way she wrote. He's upset now, thinks he showed poor judgment.

"Well, tonight she was evidently writing business letters to all these various people, making appointments for them to come and look at the stuff there, appraise things and so on. There was a stack of letters ready on her desk. One letter—to some art dealer—she decided to mail tonight. Had she said anything about picture dealers to you?"

"We talked about pictures."

"That's it, then; she couldn't wait to get things going. She put on a coat and tied a woollen scarf around her head, put the letter in her pocket, and started out with it. Well, she was an old lady, Ashbury thinks she must have been seventy-five years old anyway."

"She was."

"There you are. Old people—half the time they're living in the past, and Miss Paxton may have been overdoing it, working too hard on her lists and her correspondence. She used to visit there when the house had the old stoop and the old front door, and tonight she may have forgotten all about the changes. She grabbed up the letter she wanted to mail, put on her coat and her scarf, trotted down the hall, opened one of the old doors and walked out and through the railing. The rail was rusted loose in its sockets, it flattened right down. She took the ten-foot drop, landed here." Nordhall placed a hand flat on his head, just above the hairline and to the left. "Parietal bone crushed. She must have died instantly. Skull brittle—old bones."

Gamadge lighted his cigarette and put it in his mouth.

"It's a kind of a desert up there at that hour, and in cold weather," said Nordhall. "Patrolman says he sometimes doesn't meet anybody up along that way around nine o'clock for over half a mile. People either at home, or still out somewhere. Dark, too—private houses both sides of the way, some empty, like the Ashbury house was. She was found at fourteen and a half minutes past nine, and as luck would have it, by a doctor—name's Barber, he lives in the big apartment on the next corner north, and he was walking home from seeing a patient down the Avenue. He had to stay with the body for six minutes before anybody came by. He says she'd been dead for about say fifteen minutes when he found her, perhaps a little less.

"Barber sent this passer-by up to the apartment to telephone. When the police surgeon got there he more or less agreed with Barber about the time of the accident, but you know what those fellers are. Our doc says she could have been dead less than a quarter of an hour; cold night, aged victim, and of course—but he don't know that's influencing him—the fact that she was lying there on a public street.

"But some people would walk by; you know that, too. Anything not to be delayed away from a date or mixed up in an investigation.

"The body's at the mortuary, but Ashbury wanted her sent to a first class place in the morning. We picked Buckley's—you know Buckley's; no better place in town. She'll be buried in her own family plot in Tarrytown. They tell us up there that she had mighty few friends left in the vicinity, and no relatives."

After a pause Gamadge said: "Clara's away, you know; but anything I can do—"

"If Mrs. Gamadge was here I might ask her to go up tomorrow and see about getting the old lady's things packed up—Ashbury wants to close up the house again till he can make other arrangements, and he don't want Miss Paxton's things mixed up with Ashbury stuff. He said never mind, he'd think up something, but if we could fix it up for him—tough, though, getting a responsible party to do the work at short notice; any notice."

"Miss Paxton had a respectable kind of part-time woman," said Gamadge. "I could oversee her, if she'll do the job. She's there in the afternoons from three to five."

"Know her name?" Nordhall was opening the little red address book.

"A Mrs. Keate, I think."

"Here she is, and of course no telephone. They never have a telephone they can use in those rooming houses. But what do we need the address for? She'll be coming anyway. Even if she sees the news in the paper, she'll be coming for her pay. Unless she was paid every day? That's unlikely. You couldn't go up there and meet her tomorrow, could you, and get the job done and settle up? We'll put it on Ashbury's bill."

"I'll go, of course."

"You could write to her, but sometimes they get started for the day before the postman gets there."

"I'll go. How much do they get? Seventy-five an hour now?"

"I hope to God they haven't gone up. You might turn off the oil furnace and lock the windows. Mighty nice of you." Nordhall again referred to the file on Miss Paxton. "The handbag has thirty-odd dollars in it, we're keeping it for the present until we know what to do with it. She had some jewelry on her—old-fashioned stuff, old watch and chain. You might look for other valuables while you're there. We have Miss Paxton's latchkey; better have it, in case the cleaning woman doesn't come. I'll get it to you."

"Miss Paxton told me she had no other valuables than what she wore."

"All right then." Nordhall looked relieved. "Glad you showed up after all. You know when they called me, damned if I wasn't afraid you thought there was something wrong with the accident."

"Everything's wrong with it."

Nordhall threw himself back in his chair. "Oh, for Heaven's sake."

Gamadge sat up, leaned his arms on the desk, and pointed his cigarette at Nordhall. "Miss Paxton was as likely to walk out of the wrong door as you are."

"That's what you think. Gamadge—"

"She was killed. But nobody can be sure that a ten-foot drop or a much longer drop will kill anybody, so she wasn't killed by falling from the balcony; she wasn't killed by a fall."

Nordhall sat scowling at him.

"She had a coat on when she was found, didn't she?" asked Gamadge. "Her head was tied up in a woollen scarf?"

"Coat with a fur collar," barked Nordhall, "purple woollen scarf."

"She kept a golf cape in her sitting room for just such short trips. She didn't like stairs, and there probably wasn't a coat closet on that drawing-room floor. She put the golf cape on when she came out on her balcony this afternoon to see me off. Why should she go upstairs and get a coat to mail a letter at the corner?"

"I never heard anything thinner. It's the thinnest piece of guesswork—"

"I'll tell you something she wouldn't wear, to mail a letter or to go anywhere else. She wouldn't wear a woollen scarf on her head. Not on your life she wouldn't. A golf cape, yes—they were worn when she was young, worn by people like herself. A knitted scarf? No. Not even in the country. Only very poor old people wore those in Miss Paxton's young days. You will remind me of 'fascinators'—"

"No," said Nordhall stonily, "I won't."

"If you did, I should reply that an old lady like Miss Paxton would never take up that fashion again, any more than she'd wear other youthful accessories of her own youth—even if they came into style for the moment. To her a good golf cape couldn't go out of fashion."

"Kids wear those woollen scarfs now."

"She wouldn't take up a kid fashion."

"You seem to know," said Nordhall, whose face wore an obstinate expression not far removed from boredom.

"I know why a woollen scarf was wrapped round her head. But it's foolish for me to give you the thing like this; naturally you want facts first—I'll give you some of those."

Long before Gamadge had arrived at the bullet which Harold had dug out of the woodwork, or had handed it across the desk, Nordhall was also leaning forward with his elbows on the blotter. When Gamadge handed him the bullet he looked at it, rolled it in his fingers, and put it away. Then he went on making scrawls on a yellow pad, glancing up from them to Gamadge, looking down at them again. When Gamadge had finished the story he sat back, tore up his scrawls, and threw them into the waste basket as though he were throwing away something he had once valued but no longer had any use for; perhaps the last vestiges of his reason.

He said: "Never heard anything like it. No sense to it."

"Not much on the face of it."

"You telephone the Vance girl, she decides you're coming about the picture; three hours later Miss Paxton is dead. It's a murder that got by the police and two doctors working independently, and somebody took a lot of trouble over it; but why was it committed, with you loose and perhaps talking about Miss Paxton and this picture to a dozen people? What's the use of killing you, or trying to? There's always a chance of a slip-up on a killing, and sure enough this one didn't come off, though it must have looked to them like a sure thing.

"I can't understand why they went ahead with the Paxton murder—why the killer went ahead with it. But since they did, the killer wasn't Vance."

"You mean she didn't know it was going to be done tonight?"

"Or done at all. That fits in with the way she acted when you were leaving. Suppose they dropped in a little before ten o'clock, told her Miss Paxton was dead. She'd tell them then about the appointment with you. The only chance they had was to let you go in peace, and hope for the best; hope the Paxton murder would pass for an accident after all. But they'd never—you'd think they'd never kill *you*; unless—" Nordhall's hand went suddenly to the telephone—"unless they meant to clear out."

"Harold's down there now at the corner, where he can see both entrances—there must be two. Any of them could have left by an alley before Harold ever got upstairs and told me what had happened. It was always too late to catch the ones that meant to go, Nordhall."

"I'll send a relief down anyway, send two. We'll be going down ourselves. Gamadge—what is this picture racket, anyway?"

"I haven't thought it was a picture racket since I heard that Miss Paxton was dead. I think now that the picture was velvet on the side, and bad luck for the murderer. If the picture hadn't been taken, I don't believe that Miss Paxton would ever have mentioned Miss Vance's name to me. Miss Vance was on her mind because she used to deal in magic, and the change in the picture looked rather like magic to Miss Paxton. If I'd never heard of the picture, or of Miss Vance, I might have accepted the murder as an accident myself—golf cape and knitted scarf and all; I mightn't even have noticed all that corroborative detail."

"Corroborating what?" asked Nordhall patiently.

"Lawson Ashbury left Miss Paxton a life annuity—three thousand a year."

Nordhall, relief and the beginnings of comprehension in his eye, took a cigarette out of a pack and lighted it.

"The capital ought to be something like a hundred thousand dollars," said Gamadge. "And in these circumstances the capital usually reverts to the residuary legatee when the beneficiary dies. We don't know yet, but I'm pretty sure that's the way of it in this case."

Nordhall exhaled smoke gently.

"From what Miss Paxton said," continued Gamadge, "I understood that Lawson Ashbury left his estate in thirds; a third to establish Miss Paxton's trust, a third to his son, a third to his church. Miss Paxton didn't speak of any other beneficiary who was to inherit in case of her death; she left me with the distinct impression that if it hadn't been for her,

James Ashbury would have had everything that didn't go to the church."

Nordhall drummed on the desk with the fingers of both hands; his cigarette hung from the corner of his lower lip. Then he took it out and said heavily: "The department's sold on Mr. James Ashbury. It was a person-to-person call, and I don't think there was any mistake about its being Ashbury himself. All that detail. I'll call him; but—we'll have to go a little easy on it. It sounds almost as funny this way." He looked at Gamadge.

"Yes, funny."

"Send a gunman to do the job? Let all these other people in on it? You think they were in on it, whatever it is."

"They had some understanding."

"Perhaps—I wonder who else is interested? Ashbury has a wife and a son and daughter, you say."

"Yes. I'm beginning to think I met the son and the daughter this evening."

"I'll be—you mean Higgs and Simpson?"

"False names."

"You thought so right away, and the Vance girl called Simpson Jim. I suppose"—Nordhall looked hopeful—"the Spiker woman couldn't be Mrs. Ashbury?"

"Hardly." Gamadge smiled.

"I'll get those men posted, anyway." Nordhall talked into the telephone. Then he pushed it away from him and eyed Gamadge humorously. "Now you might as well go ahead and tell me all about the Paxton murder."

"You're ready for that now, are you?"

"Go right ahead. She would have worn her golf cape, she wouldn't have worn a knitted scarf. What's the rest of it?"

CHAPTER EIGHT

Portable Flat Surfaces

"**I** ASSURE YOU," said Gamadge, "that this murder was meant to be the perfect crime, and that it was in fact an almost perfect crime. It was never cooked up on the spur of the moment, in desperation, because I had appeared on the scene and requested an audience with Miss Iris Vance. I agree with you that Miss Vance is therefore out of it, except as accessory after the fact. If she had known anything about it—known that it was arranged for tonight, I mean—she would have stopped it. She would either have got in touch with the murderer or murderers, or failing that, she would have gone up there at the proper time, and waited there to call the thing off.

"But the murderer—we'll suppose that there was actually one, no matter how many accessories before the fact there may have been—the murderer had no doubt that the crime would succeed. There is very little chance, as we agreed, that taken by itself it could have failed. The background—those two front

75

doors—made the peculiarity of the alleged accident seem almost normal, by being so peculiar in itself. The psychology of the thing was convincing, doubly so after the police had had details from Mr. James Ashbury. The injury which caused death passed the scrutiny of two doctors; Miss Paxton might have been killed in that way by a ten-foot fall to the pavement."

Nordhall confirmed all this with a melancholy nod.

"But as with all competent pieces of work," continued Gamadge, "the clearer and simpler the results, the more complicated and delicate the process of creation. This was an extremely difficult murder to plan and carry out. We all know how hard it is to make murder look like accident, particularly when death results from a fall. Such falls are suspect; but a fall is the only convincing kind of accident which can happen to an old lady in a city house.

"The murderer can't count on the fall itself to cause death; people survive ten-foot drops, falls downstairs, unless there happens to be a fatal injury to the head or spine. The fall must be simulated.

"Why not indoors, where the lower flight ends in a mosaic pavement? Safer, you would think, to keep the whole thing indoors, and eliminate those few seconds of risky work on the street? No. The murderer preferred that risk. A fall downstairs is broken by the stairs themselves, a medical examiner might find a dozen clues to suggest that the crushed head or the broken spine couldn't have resulted from it. Our murderer didn't dare chance it."

"I wouldn't chance it myself," said Nordhall.

"The murder was committed indoors. But it had to be committed where blood could be washed away—there mustn't be any blood found indoors, not even the faintest trace of blood. Our murderer knows all about modern police techniques and laboratories. There's a mosaic pavement on the basement floor, modern and smooth as glass."

Nordhall said: "There ought to be some tiled bathrooms."

"An evening caller wouldn't have many valid excuses for

inviting Miss Paxton up two flights of stairs and into a bathroom. Much simpler to commit the murder on arrival—just inside the front door. Now we come to the golf cape and the knitted scarf."

"You told me about those. I give you those."

"I haven't told you nearly all about them. This murderer never missed the significance of the golf cape, or brought along a purple woollen scarf for fun. The golf cape simply wouldn't do."

"Why not?"

"It wouldn't protect Miss Paxton's body from the bruises she ought to have sustained from falling off a balcony."

"On her head?"

"Might have sustained; from the iron railing, from the ledge, from the pavement after the head was crushed and the body fell sideways. Old people bruise easily. Miss Paxton had no bruises because she didn't fall; I am sure that the medical examiner will tell you that she has no bruises because she was wearing a thick coat."

Nordhall said crossly: "They'll do a complete autopsy now. She won't go up to Buckley's yet awhile."

"So we arrive at the famous scarf, which I have already assured you that Miss Paxton didn't own. The murderer brought it along. Why?"

"Go ahead and save me the trouble."

"You know why now as well as I do. There must have been an effusion of blood; the medical examiner mustn't be forced to ask himself why there wasn't more blood on the pavement. He mustn't ask himself why there wasn't pavement dust in the wound, or why there was indoor dust on it. He mustn't ask himself anything."

"If that scarf was tied around her head as soon as the blow was struck there wouldn't be so much blood to get rid of indoors, either."

"All right for the scarf. The old railing, rusted out already, gets a final loosening. The leaf of the old front door is left open. The body is brought out and laid on the pavement."

"Yes, but who got into the house to find out about the loose railing and the mosaic floor and all the rest of it? Vance never did all that planning on Sunday afternoon."

"And if she didn't, who else got in to do it? And how? Well...who'd have an old latchkey?"

"James Ashbury. He could have passed it along, or it might have fallen into other hands without his knowing it. I suppose anybody could have wandered around up there day or night without Miss Paxton knowing it; any time except those two hours in the afternoon when the Keate woman was on the premises."

"The Keate woman's deaf."

"That makes it perfect. And tonight Miss Paxton had letters ready for mailing; one of them was picked up and put in her coat pocket, and it certainly made the picture look right." Nordhall paused to smile. "Miss Vance had a letter ready for mailing too, so you say. Looks as though the murder plan was in her mind, even if she didn't know when it was coming off. Well, nothing left for the party to do now but to flatten the railing, leave a door open, place the body outside, and walk off. I wouldn't say the whole job took more than fifteen minutes, would you? Wash-up and all. That makes the doctors right."

"And cuts down the time the body lay in the street to a minute or two—the time it took for the murderer to walk to the corner."

"Big risk, those last few minutes."

"A short one—and the murderer had a good view up and down."

"Still, that rail was flat and that door open while the killer was still in the house with the dead body and couldn't see out."

"Who looks up in New York at night, on a dark, quiet, empty stretch like that? There was a half-moon, and there were clouds; but nobody in New York looks at the moon, nobody but me. Not at the most magnificent Hunter's moon I ever saw in the sky. You tell somebody to look up, and they think you're crazy."

"All right, the murderer took the risk and got away with it. Now tell me," said Nordhall, his eye on Gamadge and his mouth widening into a smile, "about that other thing the murderer brought along besides the woollen scarf. Wrapped up in it perhaps, and then wrapped up in newspapers the way you brought the picture into Vance's flat. The blunt instrument."

"I've been wondering about that," admitted Gamadge.

"I should think you would. How many blunt instruments have that extent of surface without a cutting edge? It had to look like a wound she'd get on the flat of her head by hitting a pavement block."

"I know."

"It didn't make a ridge or a roughness. Mighty few blunt instruments like that, mighty few."

"Call it a portable flat surface. A portable flat surface with a handle."

"That describes it, but what was it?"

"Hanged if I know."

"It had to be swung; that blow had force behind it. It had to be broader than a hammer head, less tricky than the side of an axe, more purchase than a flatiron. It had to be just right. If it wasn't just right, then the medical examiner *would* ask himself questions. You're putting a lot of brains into this thing, and I don't mean your own."

"Yes, it was a brainy job, and a vicious one."

"There must have been a telephone call beforehand, Miss Paxton must have been ready and willing to come down and open the front door. The murderer wouldn't risk having her come out on that balcony where she might be seen if there was anybody around to see."

"She'd never have made an appointment for nine o'clock at night unless she thought she knew all about the caller. And the appointment was made after I telephoned her about the burglar alarm; otherwise she'd have mentioned the call to me. I'm pretty sure of that."

Nordhall glanced at his watch. "It's twenty-seven to one; the shank of the evening in San Francisco. I guess it's about time for a little talk with Ashbury." He pulled the telephone towards him, and motioned Gamadge to bring his chair around the desk. "Just a little talk," he said. "I haven't had official permission to scare him. Here's the number, they wrote it down in Miss Paxton's little red book."

"Let's see the address." Gamadge had moved up to Nordhall's side. Nordhall shoved the book to him and got through to the switchboard. He asked for Ashbury's San Francisco number.

After a wait a voice came from far away; it sounded like the voice of an elderly Chinese servant.

"Mrs. Ashbury? I think she retired. Mrs. Ashbury is not very well."

An operator set him right.

"Mr. Ashbury? I will call him."

Another voice spoke, a loudish, strong, self-confident voice:

"This is James Ashbury speaking."

"New York calling. Go ahead, New York."

Nordhall muttered out of the side of his mouth: "I'm betting on you, Buddy; don't you let me down." He spoke into the telephone: "Sorry to bother you again, Mr. Ashbury; this is Detective-Lieutenant Nordhall, Police Department, New York City."

"Oh—yes, Lieutenant?"

"About Miss Paxton. You've been very helpful, thought I ought to keep you posted."

"Thanks. Very good of you. Anything more I can do?"

"I wish we'd known your son and daughter were in town; we might not have had to trouble you at all."

There was a long pause. Then Ashbury said: "Oh yes.

They're on a trip. May I ask how you got in touch with them? I wasn't sure I wanted to let them know anything about the accident—they didn't know Miss Paxton. Nothing they could do."

"We made the connection through their cousin Miss Iris Vance."

"*Who?*"

"Miss Iris Vance."

"There's some mistake. They don't know her."

"They're intimate, Mr. Ashbury. Have a flat in the same apartment building."

"News to me," said the voice angrily. "I suppose the children met her somewhere. My daughter told me she was lucky enough to get a sub-lease. These young people. Never know half their plans…"

Gamadge sat forward, listening in. Nordhall cast a glance at his intent profile, and went on:

"I've had some more information on that accident, Mr. Ashbury. It might be better if you came East after all."

"Came East? Why?"

"I don't want to say much over the telephone, but there's some doubt now about the circumstances of Miss Paxton's death."

"Doubt? What do you mean? I thought—"

"From information I received, I'm not so sure now that it was an accident."

"Not an accident! You mean it was a—was a robbery? I thought she fell." There was a rasp in Ashbury's voice now.

"We're not so sure just what did happen. There'll be an adjournment of the inquest, anyhow. We might need you. Now about a plane reservation; we might help you there."

"I could manage it in a day or so, I think. I know a man in a bureau. I suppose this is really important? I'm a busy man, and my wife's not well."

"It's important, Mr. Ashbury. We'll find somewhere for you to stay when you get here. Perhaps your son and daughter could put you up."

This suggestion brought a violent negation from Ashbury: "I always go to the Roosevelt."

"It isn't so easy nowadays. But we'll find something. Oh, one moment more. Do you remember a picture—engraving— that hung in the hall of the Park Avenue house, just beyond the door of the dining room? Picture of—" he looked down at Gamadge's hasty scrawl—"of Lady Audley. By Holbein."

"I don't understand you. Engraving? I never knew one of them from another. There were a lot of pictures."

"This one was supposed to look like Mrs. Vincent Ashbury—your grandmother."

"I never heard of it. What of it?"

"Tell you when you get here. And before we ring off—do you know a friend of your son's named Bowles?"

Dead silence. Then Ashbury said slowly: "Bowles? No."

"Or a Mrs. Spiker?"

"No. Why?"

"As you say, the young people pick up a lot of funny friends nowadays. Well, good night. Be expecting you."

Ashbury mumbled something and broke the connection. Nordhall sat back in his chair to address Gamadge, his face wreathed in smiles:

"If I get in trouble about this it's worth it. But I won't get in trouble. Could I help following up when he gave himself away about the son and daughter? And the Paxton news was almost too much for him. Hear his voice afterwards?"

"What interested me was the fact that he knew Bowles and Spiker by those names."

"He knows all the false names you heard tonight. He knows all about it. He's in it up to his neck."

"But he didn't know his children knew Miss Vance, and he never heard of Lady Audley. I told you that was a side show."

"I'll believe anything you tell me now. And I'll make sure he does get on a plane, and stays on it till it gets here. Did Bantz take your car?"

"Yes."

"Ride downtown with us then."

Gamadge waited in the police car until Nordhall had conversed at length with his superiors over the telephone. At eleven minutes to one the car started, with a sergeant on the seat beside the driver and Gamadge and Nordhall behind.

"I got the green light," said Nordhall, "but I wouldn't have got it if Bantz hadn't dug the bullet out of the woodwork down there. You got me into this; now you'll have to stick around and see me through it."

"You couldn't get rid of me."

CHAPTER NINE

Missing Persons

AT ONE MINUTE past one the police car drew up in front of the old corner apartment house. Harold stood beside Gamadge's car talking to a plain-clothes man. "All right and thanks," said Gamadge. "Go on home."

"Want the car?"

"I'd better have it."

Harold walked off towards Third Avenue. Gamadge joined Nordhall in the lobby, where he was in conversation with an elderly Scot who wore trousers and a sweater over pajamas.

"The manager," said Nordhall. "Mr. Macdougal."

Macdougal returned Gamadge's nod, and went on talking:

"When your men rang me just now, sir," he said, "it was the first I knew that there had been trouble. I have my apartment in a wing at the back, on this floor; off the garden. If the tenants want me after ten o'clock at night they ring me.

We have no night porter, we've had none since Christmas of 1941. That one waited for his Christmas tips, and then he went off into Defense; so *we* didn't get any after that, not at night." He chuckled dryly.

"Need any?" asked Nordhall.

"Not until now, sir, but I don't know why. I hear it's a scandal, these rough characters getting into buildings for purposes of robbery."

"This was the gentleman that nearly got shot." Macdougal looked at Gamadge with sympathetic interest, and said tut-tut.

"You've had no complaint from the top floor or elsewhere?" asked Nordhall.

"Not a word, sir. They're very nice quiet young people on the top floor. Miss Vance has lived here for many years, most of her life; her parents lived here until they died. Mr. Vance was buried from the house. He was an artist, and Miss Vance herself does beautiful work for the magazines. You know this is a very old house, sir, one of the first apartments ever to go up in New York. One gentleman here was telling me that his grandfather had the apartment he has now. Our tenants don't like change."

"Don't like to use latchkeys at night, either," suggested Nordhall.

"No sir, it annoys them to be locked out. I like to humor them when I can—they humor me." He gave another dry chuckle. "Very few complaints, they know I do my best. Quiet people we have, for the most part elderly. Writing people, theatre people, artists. Very little noise, even at the New Year there's not much laughing and going-on in the halls."

Nordhall glanced up into the shadows. "Sounds like a nice place. Who are these friends of Miss Vance's in 5B?"

"A sublet for the holidays, they take the flat by the month, I understand. Miss Vance knows the lady and gentleman that live there. Mr. and Mrs. Seaward; fine people. They went to

North Carolina for the winter, and Miss Vance asked them as a favor to let Mr. and Miss Ashbury stay here while they were in New York."

"When did they come?"

"Just a week ago. Last Tuesday. They're quite in love with the house; they're like all the tenants—they appreciate charrrm," said Macdougal, "and atmospherrre."

"Well, Macdougal, I must go up and have a word with them. And one of my men will spend the night in the office, and one of them will stay where he is inside the back alley door. Don't you bother to come up, but if we need you and your passkey the sergeant here will come and get you. The flat might possibly be empty."

"Well, sir," said Macdougal equably, "you know the law. It's not so easy to get into an empty apartment, even if you have a passkey. Any noise, even dogs, and you have to apply to the Board of Health. No policeman will go in."

"This was attempted murder, Macdougal."

"Well, sir, you know best."

The top floor was quiet and dim; one unshaded bulb of low power lighted it. Miss Vance's door was ajar.

"Visiting," said Nordhall. He and Gamadge went into the flat, while the sergeant stood guard at the head of the stairs. They walked through it, Gamadge in Nordhall's wake. When they left, Gamadge shut the door behind him.

Nordhall glanced over his shoulder when he heard it close. "Plugging up the foxholes, are you?" He went over and opened the fire door. Gamadge joined him in his survey of cement stairs going down and a wooden ladder leading up to the trap in the roof. The ladder was askew.

"Somebody ran for it," said Nordhall. "Banged into the ladder. Didn't climb—the trap's bolted."

He led the way along the hall to 5B, and pushed the bell. "If Vance is visiting here," he said, "that means they're still up. Talking it over. What you bet it was Bowles went by the fire stairs?"

"I wouldn't bet."

"Can't get it through my head how Ashbury could hire a thug and let his children in on it. And they let Vance in." He pushed the bell again, and rapped on the door. "And somebody let Spiker in on it, too."

"Quite a gang," agreed Gamadge.

"And a murder racket!" Nordhall lifted his fist to pound on the door, when it opened. Young Ashbury stood looking at the visitors woodenly.

"Glad we didn't have to get you out of bed," said Nordhall. "You all might have been sound asleep, time it took you to get the door opened up."

"A few seconds," said Ashbury.

"We won't argue it. I'm Nordhall, Detective-Lieutenant in Homicide."

Ashbury stood away from the door; his eyes moved to the inner, lighted end of the passage.

"And you know this gentleman," said Nordhall. "Perhaps I'd better introduce you all over again though; he thought your name was Simpson."

"Part of the joke."

"It ended up by not being such a joke for Mr. Gamadge. We'll talk about the joke with the ladies present. Now listen, Mr. Ashbury"—as the young man seemed about to protest—"you knew very well that we were coming down here to talk to you all. So let's get ahead with it."

Ashbury's sister had appeared at the end of the passage; Iris Vance was behind her, just visible as a white and disembodied face under a halo of red.

Miss Ashbury said: "Then what we heard must have been a shot, Jim." She addressed Nordhall with cold reserve: "We didn't know."

"Tell me all about it." Nordhall walked forward, past Ashbury; Gamadge followed him. The two women stood aside, and then they and Ashbury came into the big living room too. The sergeant remained beside the outer door.

Nordhall stopped abruptly and looked about him. It was a formal room, well-furnished and rather sombre, with a framed oil landscape over the mantel, mahogany furniture, a big oriental rug. The original owners had left it a little bare, and the Ashburys had not disordered it with personal belongings. It had in fact no signs of tenancy except for some newspapers and magazines on a side table.

Nordhall had not been looking at the room. He asked: "Well, where's the man going under the name of Bowles? Where's the woman called Spiker?"

Ashbury said after a moment: "I don't know why you should think those were false names."

"You don't?" Nordhall swung to stare at him.

"No. We didn't use our names—I mean our family name—because Mr. Gamadge said he knew Miss Paxton, and we hadn't been up to see her. We were afraid she'd think it was funny."

"*I* think it's funny. Where's Bowles?"

"They left long ago."

The Ashbury girl stepped forward. Her brother said: "Don't mix in this, Janet."

"I want to know whether we really did hear a shot."

"Yes," said Nordhall, looking at her with a sardonic smile. "You really did."

"Because Mr. Bowles went out after we heard it, and we haven't seen him since."

"Went out because he heard a shot?"

"I suppose so. This is exactly what happened." She stood in front of Nordhall, looking quietly at him, with a kind of steely calm that might hide anything: "We left Iris Vance's flat as soon as this Mr. Gamadge had gone, and we came here—all of us but Iris. My brother and Mrs. Spiker and I came straight through to the kitchen for drinks. We left Mr. Bowles in the front hall, just inside the door. He was putting his coat on; he said he had to go as soon as he'd had a highball."

"A straight rye," her brother corrected her.

"Oh yes. A straight rye. The kitchen is down that passage, you can't hear what goes on in the outside hall when you're there; but we heard something, some kind of crash. We wondered what it was, and my brother thought it almost sounded like a shot. We came back here, and Mr. Bowles had gone."

"And the funny thing about it," said Nordhall, still ferociously genial, "is that he left by the fire stairs. Because Mr. Gamadge and his friend were on the stairs, a flight and a half down."

Ashbury came up to her and put a hand on her arm. "Why doesn't Mr. Gamadge tell you what happened out there?" he asked Nordhall.

"He doesn't know. If his friend hadn't been downstairs—with *his* gun—Mr. Gamadge would have been shot in the back. Shot dead."

Iris Vance murmured in a spectral voice: "This isn't a good neighborhood."

"Evidently not. I'll say it's a bad one. So Mr. Bowles ran after some thug, did he? That the way you all want it?"

Janet Ashbury turned away. "That's all we know." She went across the room and sat down on a bench under the windows.

Ashbury said: "Sit down, Iris." He moved one of the chairs that stood in front of the fire; she sank into it, and he stood behind it with his hands on the chair back.

"Well, I'm glad that mystery's cleared up," said Nordhall. "I mean the mystery of why none of you bothered to find out why there'd been a crash in the hall. Miss Vance was listening to the elevated train. Bowles hasn't called up to say he caught the party that fired at Mr. Gamadge—or was going to fire at him."

"I don't understand what did happen," said Ashbury.

"We won't waste time over it. How can I get in touch with your friend Bowles and Mrs. Spiker?"

Ashbury said: "I don't know where Bowles is staying."

"You don't?"

"I hardly know him. I met him in a bar."

"You met him at a bar, and brought him home with you to play a joke on Mr. Gamadge?"

"I brought him home with me. We heard about Mr. Gamadge afterwards from Miss Vance."

Nordhall stood looking at him.

"He's all right," said Ashbury. "He's an oil salesman, I think he lives in Dallas. I'm interested in oil myself, I'm going into that business. I knew Janet was having a buffet supper, and I brought him along. I bring friends, she brings friends. Nothing formal about the way we live."

"And Mrs. Spiker—who brought *her* home with them?"

Iris Vance said: "She came to see me. She's an agent for a cosmetics firm; I met her through some advertising people once. She had some idea she wanted to work out with me for her firm. I should have divided the money with her, of course, if they'd taken up her idea and I'd drawn a picture."

"And she had supper here too?"

"Yes."

"You told Mr. Gamadge when he called you up this afternoon that you were going out to dinner."

"I meant supper here."

"Well, that places all five of you, does it, safe and sound in this apartment here until say nine o'clock?"

"Until nearly ten," said Ashbury, "when we moved down the hall."

"Fine. Now I'll just try and get hold of Mrs. Spiker. Unless Miss Vance doesn't know where she is? Or unless she's left town?"

"She's staying at the Hambledon on Seventh Avenue."

"Well, that's a nice quiet commercial hotel. What's her full name?"

"Miriam Spiker. She's a widow. I don't know her by her married name."

Nordhall, with a glance that included them all, a glance of savage amusement, went to a telephone which stood on the table with the magazines. He picked up the directory from its shelf below, found his number and dialed. Gamadge, who stood leaning against the wall near the entrance archway, thought he had never seen people wait more quietly than those three waited while Nordhall got the Hambledon.

"Mrs. Miriam Spiker, please," said Nordhall. "Oh. When? About one?... That's too bad. Thanks."

He put down the receiver and turned. "Isn't that too bad?" he said. "Mrs. Spiker left the Hambledon at about one o'clock—checked out. Now let's just make a guess about that. We've got a timetable to work from." He stood propped against the edge of the table, looking from one to the other of the Ashburys, and from them to Iris Vance.

"Let's see. Mr. Gamadge left here around eleven, and Mrs. Spiker left soon afterwards. She started packing up right away. I finished talking to your father, long distance, at about twenty-two minutes to one. He called you up here, of course, soon as we finished talking. Say he got you in ten minutes; that's quick work, but it can happen. The minute he gave you the news about Miss Paxton's adjourned inquest and all that, you called Mrs. Spiker at the Hambledon. She was all ready to go, and she made it—checked right out. Perhaps you called Bowles too. Shame there's no switchboard here, but we can check the long distance call."

Ashbury cleared his throat. He said: "My father did call us up, of course."

"We can check your call to the Hambledon."

"You might check on *a* call to the Hambledon," said Ashbury. "I suppose Mrs. Spiker has her own affairs to attend to."

"And they get her out of her hotel, unexpectedly, in the middle of the night. Mr. Ashbury, your father tells me he didn't know you knew Miss Vance."

"He didn't know."

"How was that?"

"There was some absurd old family feud. I looked Iris up when I was East at college, and Janet met her then too. We saw no reason why we shouldn't know our only relation—the only one in New York, the only one in fact except Miss Paxton in Tarrytown. I was going to tell Dad when we got home."

"Why tell him now?"

"Because Iris and I are engaged to be married."

Nordhall's eyes went to her. "That makes her practically one of the family, the immediate family, not merely a cousin."

Ashbury said: "That's really why we gave false names tonight. I mean it's the principal reason. We didn't want it getting around to Miss Paxton—that we knew Iris. Not until we had a chance to tell my father ourselves."

"He didn't seem any too pleased when I told him."

"Because he thought Iris was a medium. I couldn't explain about her being an artist, because I wasn't supposed to know her or anything about her." Ashbury shifted his hands on the chair back. "These ideas older people have— you can't change them in a minute." He went on after a pause: "We don't know anything about that picture—that engraving Mr. Gamadge brought in. It didn't mean a thing to us; it doesn't yet."

"And it doesn't matter now," said Nordhall. "Does it? Because the only person that knew it was a substitution can't talk now. She's dead."

Ashbury, bent forward a little, stared at him vacantly. Iris Vance spoke in that dying, far-off voice: "When Mr. Ashbury told us so over the telephone we could hardly believe him."

"No, it's a funny kind of coincidence," said Nordhall. "Funny series of events. Miss Paxton gets Mr. Gamadge to come here about a picture; she's dead before he arrives, and an hour later he's all but murdered himself as he's leaving your place. Nobody here knows about that, nobody here knows where Bowles and Mrs. Spiker got to, Mrs. Spiker checked out of her hotel as soon as she heard about Miss Paxton's inquest being adjourned.

"You know what's going to look even funnier when it gets to the newspapers? Your father didn't tell us, when we first called him up, that you were in New York. We got that another way. If Mr. Gamadge hadn't made up his mind that those two pictures had been switched, your names and Miss Vance's name and Bowles and Mrs. Spiker would never have been heard of in connection with Miss Paxton's death.

"Now I'll be frank with you. We're not going to give any of it to the newspapers till your father gets here and we have a talk with him; unless he's too long getting here, and I don't think he will be. But until he arrives we'll have to check up on you—that's routine—and see that you don't disappear too.

"For tonight, all I suggest is a search. Just routine, and more or less of a joke in the circumstances, but we have the bullet that didn't hit Mr. Gamadge, and we wouldn't be acting sensibly if we didn't at least look for the gun it came out of. I asked them to send a policewoman down—she ought to be here now. Any objection? I have no warrant, but you might like it better this way, instead of all going downtown and waiting around there till I get one. More privacy this way—you'll like that."

Janet Ashbury was looking at her brother, her dark eyes fiery. He said: "Better take it, Jane. What do you and Iris care?"

"That's right," said Nordhall. "What do you care?" He went out into the passage, spoke to the sergeant, and came back. The sergeant let himself out of the flat, closing the door quietly after him.

"Just a question or two more," said Nordhall. "What business is your father in, Mr. Ashbury?"

"None just at present."

"What business was he in?"

"Importer."

"Where from?"

"China, Japan, East Indies, and so forth."

"War retired him?"

"Temporarily."

"What do you do? You said something about oil."

"I'm looking around. Just out of the army."

"Branch?"

"Air. I didn't get overseas."

Silence fell. Ashbury went and sat down beside his sister. Nobody said anything more until the doorbell rang. Nordhall let the sergeant and a stocky woman into the flat; Gamadge passed them, murmured that he was going home, and went into the hall.

He descended the stairs in a crablike manner, one hand clasping Harold's Colt and his head turned back over his shoulder. But all the flat doors and the fire doors remained shut, and he reached the lobby without accident. He said good night to the plain-clothes man, and got into his car.

CHAPTER TEN

Out From Under

GAMADGE'S FAVORITE CLUB, a small but rather famous one, had its quarters in a remodeled private house behind Gamadge's own, on the next street South. The club-house had been planned and finished inside and out by a master, long since dead. As Gamadge's grandfather had been a charter member, and as he and Gamadge's father had done an immense amount of thankless work for it on committees and boards, a privilege had been granted them and extended to Gamadge himself—the privilege of a connecting gate between the club's rear premises and the Gamadge back yard.

Gamadge used this gate tonight. He garaged his car in the private building adjoining the clubhouse, and retaining his keys in his hand, went up the white front steps. The night porter let him in—a grandfatherly person in dark blue.

"I'm just taking the short cut home, Parsons."

"Yes, sir." Parsons never even *thought* questions about a member's activities—much less asked them.

He saw Gamadge along the black-and-white marble pavement of the hall, through to the terrace, and watched him down the steps and past the bare shrubs and trimmed evergreens to the green gate in the white fence.

"Got your key, sir?"

"I always have my key." It was the only one. Gamadge would have been as likely to lose his car key, his latchkey, or the key to his safe deposit box.

"Good night, sir."

"Good night, Parsons. Thank you."

"'*kyou*, sir." Parsons had come from the land of good clubs, and knew how to talk.

Gamadge went through into his wintry garden, locked the gate after him, and found his way to the basement door. He had no key to this, and was forced to pound on it.

Old Theodore, sketchily clad, peeped out at him and then grudgingly opened the door just wide enough for Gamadge to come in.

"You didn't tell me you're goin' play cards all night," grumbled Theodore. "What's the use of a gate key and no door key?"

"I didn't know I was going to play cards all night." Gamadge climbed the stairs to the first floor. Harold met him at the door of the laboratory.

"Hello," he said. "Back way?"

"Well, after all, somebody did show signs of wanting my blood."

"That's so."

"*I* don't want any more shooting."

"Regular war, is it?"

"To the knife, I should say. Shouldn't you?"

They went into the laboratory and sat down at the table where Harold had been working at some mathematical formulae. Gamadge described the events of the night since they had parted two hours earlier. It was now ten minutes of two.

When he had finished, Harold said: "Bowles and Spiker on the loose. Why shoot you? Why shoot *you*?"

"Did we ever know?"

"Of course without you there'd be no first-hand witness to what Miss Paxton said about the picture."

"There's that."

"It always goes back to the picture." Harold smiled. "I put it up on the mantelpiece in the library. Like to look at it."

"It's a nice thing."

"Funny case. Funny collection of people."

"Yes. Know how I feel about it?"

"Stumped."

"I feel as if every step I took was a step down. The only way to go is down. And the farther down, the harder it is to breathe the air."

"I'm not much on these allegories," said Harold, "but I've been down in old cellars myself."

"Damp ones," said Gamadge. "Dirt floor, anything you find there covered with mold."

"Plenty of rats, too."

"Rats, of course. Nordhall is trying to scare something out of those three; he won't do it. He'll never do it."

"Don't they scare?"

"They're all terrified. Won't do Nordhall any good."

Harold reflected. Then he said: "Trouble is, a hundred thousand dollars doesn't cut so good six ways. Wait a minute—Vance and young Ashbury would count as one. Five ways. But twenty thousand isn't so much for people like that to commit a murder like that for. Of course Bowles and Spiker both could be on salary, but if they're going to risk taking the rap I should think they'd come high."

There was a ring at the front door, faintly heard from the back of the house. Gamadge rose. "I'll spare Theodore's feelings," he said. "You shout down if he comes and tell him to go back to bed."

"Would that be Nordhall?"

"Don't know."

"Hadn't I better take it?"

"I'll keep the chain on."

Gamadge opened the door to the extent of the chain, kept behind it, and asked: "Who is it this time of night?"

"Misther Gamadge…"

"It's you, Connell?" Gamadge took the chain off and opened the door wide. The patrolman on the beat stood there, a vast officer well known to Gamadge. His red face wore such a strange expression that the other was startled. "What's the trouble, Connell? Aren't you well?"

Connell did not reply, but he closed immense fingers on Gamadge's upper arm and drew him out into the cold and dark of the night. The grip was meant to be a friendly one; it felt like the clasp of half a pair of ice tongs.

"What's wrong?" Gamadge searched the face of Connell, which was still distorted into a grimace.

"Take a luk."

Propelled to the railing, Gamadge obediently looked down into the area. At first glance he might have thought it was some large, furry animal that crouched for shelter or safety against the basement gate; but Connell put on his torch.

"My God." Gamadge, hands on the rail, stared down. It was a woman in a fur coat, and half of her face was a dark mask, glistening wet.

"She's dead, sir. Will you go down there and wait while I put in the call?"

"Yes; but—"

"Just found her, one minute after two o'clock. She might have run in to get away from somebody." He added: "I think she's shot. You wouldn't have heard it?"

"Bantz and I were back in the laboratory."

Connell and Gamadge went down to the street. Connell lumbered to the corner, Gamadge went down and stood in the area in front of Mrs. Spiker. She had lost her fancy hat—no, it was half under her.

Harold looked out, peered over the rail. He met Gamadge's eyes in silence. Then he said: "Wasn't here when I came home—about one-twenty."

Gamadge said: "She didn't quite make it. It's the Spiker woman."

"Somebody waiting here for you, got her instead?"

"Looks that way."

"She was getting out from under?"

"Looks that way."

"Don't stand out here like a dummy with Bowles perhaps in the next area."

"I have your gun. Go and telephone Nordhall, stay there till you get him."

Harold disappeared into the house; Gamadge stood beside the dead woman, facing the street. Now and then he glanced down at the dabbled, brassy hair, the glimpse of painted cheek, the bright earring. Poor woman, he thought, she must have been clear of the murder or she'd never have tried to come to me...As soon as she heard from the Ashburys—that Miss Paxton was dead—she decided to quit. Went somewhere—all-night checking office or station locker—and got rid of her luggage, then came up here.

Connell came back, the squad cars came, and Nordhall came in their wake. For the next two hours Gamadge's office and laboratory became temporary headquarters for Homicide detail; never in their official lives had such a convenience been theirs, and they took full advantage of it.

The mortal remains of Mrs. Miriam Spiker—if that was her name—were placed under a bright light on a laboratory work table, where the medical examiner conducted a pre-autopsy examination. Old Theodore, fully dressed and trembling with indignation, came up from his basement to protest. Two bullets from a .32 gun were extracted and put under the microscope. The body was fingerprinted. An urgent general call went out for a Mr. Bowles, redescribed by Gamadge. The Hambledon Hotel was able to say only that Mrs.

Spiker had checked in on Tuesday, the week before, and had left that night with a suitcase. She had carried it herself, and nobody had seen her take a cab. Miss Iris Vance, called to the telephone, but not informed of Mrs. Spiker's death, confessed that she had taken Mrs. Spiker more or less on trust. She had met her at a big advertiser's convention, where anybody might go, and had never heard of the cosmetics firm—Jones & Jones—which Mrs. Spiker had given out as her employers.

"And nobody else ever heard of them, either," said Nordhall. "Vance ought to be in a cell. She's told more lies this evening than all the rest of them put together."

But Nordhall only said that because he was annoyed; Mrs. Spiker's handbag had disappeared.

A final unearthly touch was supplied to the proceedings by Gamadge's cat Martin, who ran back and forth between office and laboratory, as if on some urgent business of his own, getting under everybody's feet and paying no attention to anyone.

The Press got in. They were told that the deceased was a Mrs. Miriam Spiker, supposed to be a cosmetics agent, and that she had probably been followed away from some bar and killed and robbed. Nobody intimated that anything but blind chance had placed her in Gamadge's areaway; nobody but one young man, a newsman acquainted with Gamadge, who cornered the latter in his library to suggest—in sarcasm—that Gamadge had become a Mad Scientist in the best tradition, and had taken to supplying himself with cases for criminological investigation. Gamadge supplied him with what he came for—a drink—and got rid of him.

At something after three o'clock Nordhall joined Gamadge and Harold in the library. He told them that Mrs. Spiker had been shot twice at close range, both bullets lodging in the skull; and the bullets had come from the gun that had been aimed at Gamadge over the stair rail.

"Bantz dug their mate out of the woodwork down there," he said. "What do you carry around with you, Gamadge, besides an outsize sense of self-preservation? What's your lucky number? Give the rest of us a break."

"There's no luck to it. Harold went to a lot of trouble nursemaiding me down at Vance's place, and I came home by way of the Club."

"I know, but damn it, you have Harold and you have that club. As a matter of fact I'm not so sure you're right about that ambush in front. I agree with you that Spiker was coming to see you for ratting purposes, and I'm inclined to agree with you about that letting her out as a principal in the Paxton murder. If she came to see you, she thought you could help her out from under; she must have known you couldn't and wouldn't do it if she confessed to a murder job."

"She took the whole thing more lightly than the rest of them did this evening—when I called on Miss Vance with the picture. That's one of the things that's been puzzling me so much—how she could have taken it as she did if she knew Miss Paxton was lying dead uptown."

"I'll give you all that; but why couldn't she have gone somewhere and called Bowles up from a pay station after she left the Hambledon, talked things over with him? Then he got some idea she was getting out, and trailed her up here and caught up with her? He'd have found out where you lived."

"She didn't have much time."

"She had an hour. You're counting in the time it took her to get rid of her bag, but suppose she left it with Bowles?"

"She might have done that."

"Come to think of it, it doesn't seem likely that she'd go and talk to a killer like Bowles if she meant to blow the whole thing. And my idea is that when that shooting went wrong on the Vance stairs it knocked all their plans out; if she was packing to quit the Hambledon, Bowles was checking out of his place too. How would she get in touch with him unless she knew he had another hideaway? He didn't call her at the Hambledon—they say she only had one call this evening, and that was from the Ashburys."

"But they didn't listen in on it, I gather."

"No, and even if they had what good would that do us? Those people must have a code, they couldn't work without one, not long distance from San Francisco. We'll check on James Ashbury's call to them tomorrow. And I may have something more on him—the Commissioner has friends on a San Francisco paper. See you in the morning." Nordhall rose.

"If you come before noon you'll have to break in," said Gamadge.

"Noon suits me. Thanks for everything; you treated the boys right."

"I only wish I could have kept that unfortunate woman here and given her a funeral. I rather liked her," said Gamadge gloomily.

"She darn near helped fix up a funeral for you."

Nordhall went home. Harold, on his way up to bed, paused to ask: "Another step down?"

"Another long step down."

"Only Bowles probably took things into his own hands this time. I don't believe," said Harold, in the doorway, "that he called up headquarters for permission to rub out Mrs. Spiker. That's the trouble with hiring gunmen, they think there's only one answer to a problem."

"Don't you suppose that the Ashburys will cover up for this murder too?"

"That's so. The air is getting thicker, isn't it? And nothing you could call evidence yet."

"Nothing you could call proof, anyway."

Harold went upstairs. Gamadge waited until the house was quiet, and empty of strangers; then he put on his hat, coat and gloves, reconnoitred at the front door, and let himself out of the house.

CHAPTER ELEVEN

But Will They Come

GAMADGE WALKED DOWN to Fifty-ninth Street, and took the subway to Eighteenth. He emerged, and walked south and east to the Vance apartment house. A plain-clothes man—the one Gamadge had met earlier that evening—sat in the office reading a magazine. He looked up and nodded. "You back again? Nordhall left long ago."

"I had to come back. Something I forgot."

"Up there? Want me to go along?"

"No thanks."

"All quiet, I guess. All sewed up. Man in back, and there's going to be three on the day shift."

"One for each?"

"That's right. The subjects can go out, but we'll be right after them in case they try to make any contacts—Bowles or Spiker."

"I'd like to see the back premises."

"Go ahead. Tell the guy there that I sent you—Lugan. He's Weinberg."

Gamadge went out to the street again and around the corner to Third Avenue. Between the apartment house and a grocery store he found the alley, a flagged path dark as night itself. Gamadge went along it, bumped into ashcans, and circled them to emerge on a square of garden. He came back and pounded on a door.

A face looked out. Gamadge said: "Weinberg? Lugan sent me around here. I was with Lieutenant Nordhall."

"Gamadge," said Weinberg. "I saw you."

"I was interested in the layout back here."

"It's nothing." Weinberg let Gamadge in and closed and bolted the door. They stood on a landing; cement steps went up and down, and behind the plain-clothes man there was another door, in the wall.

"Footprints?" asked Gamadge.

"They don't seem to take. We didn't find any. Or else this Bowles floats."

Gamadge laughed politely and went through the door into the lobby. He climbed from landing to dim landing, arrived at the top floor, and turned to Apartment 5A. He stood up against the door and very gently turned the knob. The door opened.

All was silent, but every light seemed to be on in the living room. He walked softly forward. The left-hand wall of the living room came into sight. On a studio couch there Iris Vance now lay asleep. She was fully dressed, and the light Indian blanket which had covered her was flung back and sliding to the floor. The flat was very cold.

Gamadge tiptoed across the room and down the inner passage. Nobody. He came back, retreated into the outer hall, closed the door, and rang.

In a few moments he heard her voice: "What is it?"

"Gamadge. Nothing wrong, Miss Vance. I wanted to speak to you."

She opened the door a little way and stood looking up at him and shivering.

"You're frozen," said Gamadge. "Why didn't you go to bed?"

She opened the door wider, and he came past her into the living room and stood looking at the studio couch and frowning. "Been spending the night there? What for? Never mind now; I'll just thaw you out a little first."

He went over to the fireplace, kindled a fire, piled on wood, and then picked up the whiskey bottle which still stood on the table, half full. He went down the inner passage to the kitchen, Iris Vance following him with uncertain steps.

Gamadge lighted a gas burner on the stove, found a saucepan, poured whiskey into it, put the pan on the flame, and began to hunt along shelves and in cupboards.

"Sugar? Right in front of my eyes. Knife in the drawer. Two glasses. Lemon in the icebox? Fine. We'll have a toddy. I need one myself."

"Why did you come?" Her teeth were chattering. Gamadge had thrown his hat on a kitchen chair. Now he shed his coat and put it over her shoulders. "Later," he said. "I can't talk to people while they're having a chill." He put the two steaming glasses on a tray, spoon-handles rising from them. "Especially not at four in the morning. I don't know about you, but at four in the morning, if I'm unfortunate enough to be up and about, I require artificial stimulus. The inner man doesn't supply a thing but mental and physical protest. Now some people, they tell me—bright as a button. Oh well."

He carried the tray back into the living room, set it down, took his coat off her shoulders, and pushed up a chair to the fire. When she was sitting in it, slowly sipping grog from her spoon, he pulled up another chair and sat beside her.

"In a few minutes," he said, "we'll be strong rugged characters again. Keep at it—never mind if it burns your tongue...Feeling better? So am I. Now where shall we begin? Will you tell me why you kept on all the lights and didn't dare go to bed, or shall I start the ball rolling?"

"I was frightened."

"But when people leave the lights on and can't go down dark passages to bed it means only one thing—ghost stories. Like that ghost story you told us tonight."

"Every now and then it frightens me still. And that picture—the words coming out on that picture that looks like old Mrs. Ashbury…And then people thinking I'd stolen it."

Gamadge looked at her, his glass halfway to his lips. He took a swallow, put the glass down on the flat arm of his chair, and got out his cigarettes. He lighted one for her and one for himself.

"It's an awful moment," he said, "the moment when one's early sins seem to be coming home to roost. Pain in the side—My God, my liver; how many highballs *do* I drink in a week? Seems to me I used to fairly swash them down. And so on. But you? That tap on the shoulder."

"I can feel it now."

"And I see that I'll have to find you a proof before letter of Lady Audley. Meanwhile, the thing to do in such circumstances is to keep the mind on Hotspur."

"Hotspur?"

"Surely you remember Hotspur and Glendower. Glendower says he can call spirits from the vasty deep. And what does Hotspur say, Hotspur the realist?"

"But will they come…"

"Right. And you get an unmistakable conviction that Shakespeare's talking then. He means that Glendower's the ninny, Hotspur's the sensible man."

"It doesn't mean they won't come."

Gamadge turned his head to look at her severely. "Of all the feeble interpretations I ever heard, that's the feeblest. It does mean they won't come."

"It only asks."

"Miss Vance, I beg of you, don't make me despair of your intelligence. Don't force me to tell you what you know already—the rhetorical device used there. That question expects a negative answer."

"Hotspur is only casting a doubt…"

"Miss Vance, do you seriously think that Shakespeare thought Glendower could call spirits from the vasty deep?"

"He leaves it in doubt."

Miss Vance's teeth had stopped chattering, color had come into her face, her eyes no longer looked dazed. Gamadge drained his glass and set it down. He said: "All right. He leaves it in doubt. Therefore you couldn't go to bed. That's settled, and we can go on to my reasons for coming down here tonight. In the first place, I came back to latch your front door."

"My—"

"Because I left it unlatched when Nordhall and I came here at one o'clock. The door was ajar, and we looked around your place. When I left I pushed the button that releases the latch."

She was gazing at him white-faced again.

"Because," said Gamadge, "I was afraid you might decide—or be constrained—to harbor a murderer."

She said, her lips barely moving: "There are men downstairs. Nobody could get in."

"Nobody could get in after the men were posted. But suppose our friend had never left the building? Those fire exits have doors on every landing, and the men were posted downstairs. What safer place to hide in than a place that has been searched already by the police?"

She said soundlessly: "Ridiculous."

"Is it? You're backing these people, Miss Vance, and I suppose you know what you're letting yourself in for. But are you so sure they're backing you? Miss Ashbury wanted to hang the theft of the picture on you; what if the whole family hung the murders on you?" He added: "Murder and attempted murder—mine."

"I can't imagine why you should even dream—"

"Miss Ashbury let you down once. Why not again? And why isn't Ashbury here, sitting up with you and mixing your grog?"

Tears had begun to roll down her cheeks. Gamadge felt for his handkerchief, but she produced one and dried her eyes with it.

"Is Miss Ashbury nervous too?" he asked. "Is she the one he has to sit up with?"

"With all the worry," sobbed Miss Vance, "of course they have to be together."

"Well, it's a funny thing."

"We don't understand about your being shot at, and Miss Paxton's death was an accident—even the police thought so until you—until you—"

"Miss Paxton's death was murder—cold-blooded murder, premeditated, and cruel as the grave. I came down here, secretly and in the dead of night, to beg you to tell me what you know about it. Nobody will know that you told me; it's a dangerous thing, I realize it, to inform on a murderer like this one, but you're quite safe; nobody will know."

"I don't know anything."

"And that's that." Gamadge rose. "You're locked in now, anyway; and I don't think you're going to catch cold. Would you like me to wait until you get yourself to bed?"

"If you would..."

"Sing out when you want me to put out the lights and go."

She got up and stood looking at him in confusion. "I ought to thank you."

"'Thank you, damn you.' That the way you feel?"

"It's awfully good of you to wait."

"Remember," he called after her as she went down the passage, "they will not come."

"They will not come."

Gamadge put on his coat. Miss Vance came back, holding his hat in both hands. "You left it in the kitchen."

"Thank you," said Gamadge. "I'd be tickled to death if Ashbury found it there in the morning."

She couldn't smile. She didn't even look at him again. After she had been gone a few minutes she called: "I'm all right now. Thank you."

"Good night."

He switched off the lamps and groped his way to the front door. Down in the lobby the plain-clothes man intercepted him: "Get anything?"

"No."

"They telephoned me about Spiker."

"Did they?"

"One less contact to worry about. Wonder if it'll make the morning papers."

"I shouldn't think so. She wasn't important enough."

"That's what *they* think. Funny they didn't tie you up with it."

"None of the pressmen on that job knew me from Adam—except one, and I'm afraid he'll get a wigging."

"Well, we know one thing—these three birds didn't do it. I guess they hire out that kind of work, anyway."

CHAPTER TWELVE

News Items

AT NOON NEXT day Gamadge was finishing his breakfast in the library. Harold, stretched out on the chesterfield, read aloud from the morning paper:

AGED WOMAN KILLED BY FALL

Miss Julia Paxton, a resident of Tarrytown, was the victim of an unusual accident last night when...

"Mrs. Spiker didn't make it?" asked Gamadge.

"She didn't make it." Harold looked up at Lady Audley, whom he had propped behind silver candlesticks on the chimney piece. "You'll be in the news some day," he told her. "'Titled Englishwoman abducted, impersonated by illegitimate twin.'"

Theodore, still put out by the events of the night before, appeared in the doorway. He was closely followed by Lieutenant Nordhall.

"Lieutenant Nordhall to see you," he said.

"Tell him I'm not at home."

"You tell him it ain't the law for him to come bustin' up like this. Police wait to be announced like anybody."

"I'd like a cup of coffee." Nordhall sat down in front of the fire, leaned back, and immediately sat up again to gaze at a scene displayed on the hearthrug: Martin the yellow cat lay on his side, lazily batting a paw at an all-yellow kitten. Nordhall turned to look at Gamadge in wild surmise.

"Don't ask me anything about it," said Gamadge, "I don't know. They tell me Martin got out into the yard one day and came back with the creature."

"Who says so?"

Theodore was filling another breakfast cup. He said: "Harold say so."

"I think it's a poor relation," said Harold.

"Or it might be the old feller's nominating his successor." Nordhall took the cup from Theodore's tray, his eyes still on the replica of Martin.

"His what?" asked Gamadge.

"The old feller's getting on."

"Don't, Nordhall; don't."

"You want to be realistic about these things."

"About Martin? He's only half real himself. Can't be realistic about cats."

Nordhall waited until Theodore had gone. Then he said: "I understand you made an early morning call downtown."

"Yes. Miss Vance wouldn't tell me anything."

"Angels couldn't go where you go."

"They wouldn't want to."

"Just let you in and sat and talked to you, did she?"

"Why not? She isn't afraid of me personally. She's backing the Ashburys—she's badly in love with the boy—but you and I decided that she couldn't even have known there was a murder coming off last night."

"I suppose even you didn't take it upon yourself to tell her there's been another killing?"

"Certainly not."

"Wonder if that news would have made her talk."

"No news would. At present she's in a complicated state of mind—she's being pursued by the Furies. She's had so many shocks, one on top of the other, that she thinks—or half thinks—the spirits are doing it all; to get even with her for insulting them when she was a child."

"On the level?"

"Quite. Don't forget that she was brought up by zealots."

Nordhall was getting out a folder of typed papers. "You might like to do a really useful job for us today—you and Bantz. If you're really so keen on this job."

"I'm keen on it," said Harold.

"The Ashburys are going to keep a lunch engagement at the St. Roche at one o'clock. The St. Roche is only a few blocks west of the Vance apartment house, on Fifth Avenue."

"I know where it is." Gamadge came over and sat opposite Nordhall.

"I'm just reminding you that it's within walking distance of their place. They each have a man looking out for them, of course, but if they split up they each need two. I don't have to remind you that we haven't our full quota of men yet, and the D.A. keeps reminding me that all we actually have so far is the match-up on those bullets."

"Too bad," remarked Harold.

"I know, but he's a lawyer. You know how they pick at things. The same mobster that may have aimed at Gamadge may have hung around and followed Mrs. Spiker and held her up when she came here."

"What did she come here for?" asked Harold, restraining himself.

"To talk Gamadge out of suspecting Vance stole the picture," said Nordhall. He looked up at Lady Audley. "That it?"

"That's it," said Gamadge.

"If that's like old Mrs. Ashbury, then all I can say is, old Mrs. A. had a mean, smug face and no imagination."

"The artist cr—saw his subject like that."

"But old Mrs. A. *was* like that, according to Miss Paxton. If her son Lawson was anything like that, and he probably was, I must say I wouldn't have minded playing a joke on him myself, if I'd been the Vance kid. Well, what do you say about going down to the St. Roche?"

"I won't be able to eat lunch," said Gamadge, with a sigh. "And there isn't a better lunch in town."

"I'll eat the lunch," said Harold.

"Fine. Then the Ashburys can't pull any backdoor stuff on our guys. They're young—the Ashburys—and they may think they can shake our guys off. They might at that. What we're hoping for, of course, is a contact with Bowles. We figure that they haven't heard from him at all since he lammed out after not shooting you last night."

"Afraid to telephone?"

"He'd be, in case police were at the Ashburys'; they'd be, even if they knew where he was. Too dangerous now. Anyway, that's what we hope."

"Harold and I will drive down to the St. Roche," said Gamadge. "My car's on the next street."

"That's fixed then; fine." Nordhall sorted his papers. "Now I'll tell you how far we've got. A Mr. Halsey Bowles of Dallas, Texas, checked into the Hotel Lingard on Seventh Avenue last Tuesday week, the fourth. He checked out at twelve last night."

"Nice work," said Gamadge.

"Just routine. Well, the dates make it all perfect. Bowles, Mrs. Spiker and the two Ashburys arrived here on Tuesday the fourth, a nice little party of four, on from the West for a spree. Perhaps they all came on the same train—roomettes for the Ashburys, a lower for Mrs. Spiker, an upper for Bowles. If it was a murder party they must have been pretty sure of themselves; but it looks as if Mrs. Spiker didn't know it was a murder party until you crashed in on it.

"Bowles had a big suitcase with him; he and it have faded away. We can't find Mrs. Spiker's suitcase, perhaps we never will.

"Now for our San Francisco dope, and I'm glad to say we have a good deal. Ashbury's on his way, due here tomorrow. If he tries to leave his plane he'll run into trouble. They'll be watching out for him at every stop.

"He's always had a good position in San Francisco, good socially and in business. He was always crazy about the water, had a nice little seagoing yacht, but since the war he naturally had to give that up; he's been camping instead. He has a nice house outside town, nice country house, camp in the mountains. Nothing fancy, just comfortable. Nobody's heard anything about his being hard up since the war; took it for granted he'd saved plenty of capital.

"First wife, a Miss St. Helier, California girl, came from a fine family in reduced circumstances. Killed in a motoring accident—he wasn't along. All O.K., according to what they tell us. He never does seem to be on the spot when accidents happen, does he? But he certainly doesn't seem to have gained anything by her death except his liberty. He didn't marry again till five years later—that was ten years ago. And darned if the second wife wasn't a lady in reduced circumstances too; a Miss Chauncey from St. Louis, teaching school there when he met her. They came across each other while she was on vacation, visiting friends in Burlingame."

"You must have had the social editors out of their beds at break of day," said Gamadge.

"The Commissioner got busy last night. You haven't heard the half of it."

"I'm hanging on your words."

"That's right. Well, the children were left to their own devices after their mother died, and they picked schools and colleges in the East. Never came home except vacation times, and when they were home ran around with a gay crowd. Nothing against them personally except a few tickets for driving violations and that kind of thing. Ashbury Junior was drafted into the Air Force, and was just going overseas when the surrender came.

"Now comes the interesting part—the other side of the picture, you might call it: I said Ashbury liked sailing. He was crazy on the subject, and the society bunch complained because he was always dragging the first Mrs. A. off on long cruises with him, right in the middle of the doings. She was well liked, and her friends missed her from the club dances and card parties and whatever they do. Sports, too—she never got a chance at her tennis and her golf and her riding. Always off on these cruises with Ashbury.

"After she died he didn't go around much; never cared for the regular social life, and cared less and less for it. Went camping, hunting, fishing, mostly alone with his chauffeur and some other men he hired. Then in nineteen thirty-five he met this girl from St. Louis. She was well liked too, a whiz at games and parties; but danged if he didn't start hauling her off with him on those cruises too, and when that stopped, on the camping trips. She didn't have the staying power the other one had, and she folded—lung trouble or something.

"She's been a semi-invalid ever since, more or less out of circulation; half the time in rest cures in Arizona.

"And I can't get a thing about him personally except that he's pretty fond of his own way. And it might take months to find out whether he did have capital to fall back on when his business collapsed, and whether a hundred thousand might mean something to him in cash just now. Or why," said Nordhall, folding up his papers and sitting back to look at Gamadge earnestly, "that kind of man makes love matches."

"There's a type," said Gamadge, "that would never marry a woman he couldn't patronize."

"Push around, you mean? If he's a man that has to have some well-brought-up woman entirely dependent on him—"

"He evidently isn't expected to approve of his son's love match with Miss Vance. Perhaps because she hasn't the background that suits him."

"I guess that type would be what they call conventional," said Nordhall. "On the surface, anyway." He made a face. "Doesn't sound so good to me. Well: he got three long-distance calls last night; the first one from the Department, telling him that Miss Paxton had had the accident—that went through about ten-fifteen. The third was the one I made, a little after twelve-thirty; the second came through from a pay station at something after midnight. That was Bowles, of course, saying he was checking out of the Lingard for good and sufficient reasons, and probably giving a new address.

"Ashbury made one call himself at nine minutes to one, the call to his children at the Vance apartment building. I wasn't far out."

"No."

"They're acting on his instructions. Well, that's all for Ashbury just now. About the autopsy report on Miss Paxton, there isn't a thing to show that she wasn't killed by falling from the old front door to the pavement. The pavement is still the blunt instrument, so far as the medical examiner knows, and her coat saved her from any other injuries." He smiled at Gamadge.

"I'm glad *you're* still with me," said Gamadge. "If you are."

"I am. I have the pleasure of your acquaintance." Nordhall rose. "Get going, you two, and I wish you luck."

Nordhall left. Gamadge and Harold went around to the Club garage and got the car. They drove down Fifth Avenue to the old, famous and still fashionable St. Roche, all white brick and green balconies, which faced West on a quiet corner near the Arch.

They went up the white steps. A man lounging just outside the revolving doors of the lobby put up a finger in greeting.

"Hello," said Gamadge. "You know me?"

"You was described when Lieutenant Nordhall told us you'd be down." He added: "Green eyes, good dresser, left shoulder drops."

"Could be worse. What would you have done if Bantz and I hadn't been able to come? Just played your luck?"

The plain clothes man looked surprised. "Lieutenant said you'd come."

"But that was just now, wasn't it?"

"Eight this morning, before we went on duty at that interesting old landmark over on Third."

Gamadge said: "My life's being arranged for me. This gentleman here with me is even supplying me with an endless chain of yellow cats. All right, we're here."

The plain-clothes man was evidently one of those who expect oddities in conversation. He said: "I always have a wired fox. Miss Ashbury walked in here a minute ago with her brother, me just after them, Limpeck a block behind. I'm hers, Limpeck is the Ashbury feller's. Lim's across the street there."

A little man in brown stood in the doorway across the Avenue, hugging himself against the cold.

"Can watch the side entrance from there," said the plain-clothes man. "You on Ashbury?"

"Yes, I rather think I am."

"Give Limpeck a sign."

Gamadge turned and raised his hand in salutation of his partner. The little man in brown unwrapped one arm from about himself and flapped a hand in return.

"If you're looking for lunch," said the plain-clothes man, "I may have got you in bad. The doorman's deathly afraid we're going to make a pinch; when I showed him my badge he almost cried."

The doorman, in fact, scowled a little as Gamadge and Harold came through into the lobby. They made for the news-stand on the right, which was flanked by palms; sheltered by these, they looked out over the semicircular high-ceiled place, with its red carpet, its crystal chandeliers, its white-and-gold pilastered walls.

Ashbury and his sister sat side by side on a settee almost opposite the entrance. They were motionless, and Ashbury held an afternoon paper up as though he were reading from it. Janet Ashbury sat looking straight in front of her. Gamadge would hardly have known her, she was so correct and demure. Her hair was up under a fashionable but conservative little hat, her make-up was toned down to the faintest emphasis of her natural coloring, her dress and fur cape were the perfection of youthful elegance. White gloves covered the hands that clung rigidly to the handbag on her lap, and she wore a corsage of white orchids.

Ashbury's face was hidden, his hands were trembling.

"They're getting the Spiker headlines," said Harold, and bought himself a paper.

"By the look of them," said Gamadge, "they've had a shock."

"They didn't get in touch with Bowles, then."

"What does it say?" Gamadge looked over Harold's shoulder. He read: *Woman Slain In Area. Police identify body as Mrs. Miriam Spiker, registered until last night at the Hambledon Hotel as from Cleveland, Ohio.* He asked: "Anything about me?"

"Not in this sheet. Can't you wait?"

"Morning papers will have it," said Gamadge glumly.

Ashbury had laid the paper down beside him, and was saying something to his sister without turning his head. She nodded, her eyes still on vacancy.

"They have control," said Harold.

"Didn't I mention the fact?"

There was a sudden transformation; the Ashburys stood up, their faces wreathed in smiles, as a group of four came through from the street. Two men and two women; or rather a middle-aged couple, a girl, and a young man.

The Ashburys met the group, merged with it. There were snatches of talk:

"Mother, this is Jane. Father—"

"My dear child."

"Here's Susie. Here's Jim Ashbury, Susie."

"Young Jim too? This is a great pleasure."

Kisses, handshakes, smiles, laughter.

The older man was distinguished-looking, the kind of man who has a long inheritance of brains, good living, authority. The lady who seemed to be his wife was as tall as he, handsome, pleasant of manner, beautifully dressed. The younger people did their elders justice.

"And if it isn't an engagement party, family party," said Gamadge, "I never saw one."

Harold muttered: "It's ghastly. Kind of ghastly."

"Element of incongruity," agreed Gamadge, staring for all he was worth.

"Plain ghastly. Nice topic of lunch conversation: 'There's been a little trouble, folks.'"

"Won't be mentioned."

"No. Wonder what the Ashbury girl would stick at to keep that feller and get into that family."

"I couldn't begin to compute it."

"They've brushed Vance off. She ought to be here on two counts, engaged to Ashbury and a cousin besides. They've brushed her off. She'd have been invited if these people knew about her—they'd never leave her out. Wait a minute, they're fixed for the afternoon; the man's showing them theatre tickets."

"But only five."

"Ashbury isn't going with them. He's keeping his hat and coat."

The other men went off towards the coatroom. Ashbury was shaking hands with the women, patting his sister's shoulder. The older woman was speaking to the head waiter at the dining-room rope.

"Stick with them, have your lunch, take in the show," said Gamadge hurriedly, as young Ashbury turned away, down a corridor that led past the spiral stairs. "He's going by the side entrance."

"Have a good time with Limpeck."

"Thank God the next street is westbound."

Gamadge pushed through the revolving doors and ran down the white steps. The plain-clothes man was waiting patiently at the foot of them. Mr. Limpeck was still hugging himself across the way.

"What's the matter?" The plain-clothes man seized Gamadge's elbow.

"Ashbury's leaving by the other door. Your subject is lunching with a crowd and going to a matinée."

"That's good."

Mr. Limpeck, his attention suddenly focussed on the street below him and across the avenue, gave Gamadge a fleeting glance and threaded himself a path among the traffic to the east side of the way. Gamadge went and got into his car. He leaned out of the window, watching the corner, while his engine hummed.

CHAPTER THIRTEEN

First Call—Smileys

MR. LIMPECK SCUTTLED back around the corner and up to Gamadge's car. He said: "Got a cab. Watch it, he might go West instead of up. There's nothing behind, you could back."

He stood on the running board, looking over his shoulder; then he pulled the door of the car open and bundled in, clutching the long skirts of his brown overcoat. He slammed the door. "Coming up," he said. "We have a lucky start."

A cab passed, and went on up the avenue. Gamadge started the car.

"You used to this work?" asked the little man.

"Not at all used to it."

"Thing is to try to make his lights. Takes years off a man's life, making the lights. Don't hang behind, the guy hasn't looked back. He won't now, he thinks he's made his getaway."

"I suppose you people develop a sixth sense about these things," said Gamadge modestly.

"No magic about it, just practice. This car works very sweet," he added, as they stopped behind the cab when the next red light came on. "And down this way there ain't much traffic."

They went along for blocks in safety, but at Madison Square Mr. Limpeck had anxious moments.

"These trucks," he said, "act like they was paid to give aid and comfort to fugitives. And there's the green light. Can we—that's right, take a chance, you got the spirit." He sank back relieved, exhaled a loud breath, and got out a pack of cigarettes.

"I felt a couple of years dropping off my life then," said Gamadge, skimming past a bus.

"Didn't I say? I was worried when they told me they was sending a civilian down to help out," confessed Limpeck. "Better than nothing, though. One man on a job like this—it's nothing but a gesture. Just a gesture. Then Kimball—the other guy on this Ashbury job—he told me about you being practically in the Department." He grinned up at Gamadge through smoke. "Like the big spy books. Big shot in Intelligence, *you* know, nobody knows him but the man higher up."

Gamadge laughed too.

"Six or seven people waiting to bump him off," continued Mr. Limpeck merrily, "only they don't know what the guy really looks like or who he is."

"Only in this case they all know what I look like and who I am."

Mr. Limpeck had not expected to find himself in one of his favorite plots. He said after a moment: "I thought this was only a tailing job."

"That's so."

"But if they know you I'd better do the close-ups. I understand this Ashbury is going to try to contact a killer named Bowles?"

"That's the general idea."

"I never heard of any crook named Bowles."

"He's supposed to be a Westerner, and Bowles may be a false name."

"If he's a Westerner he probably don't know me, anyway. You met him?"

"Last night."

"Don't say. Look out, here we go."

They were now in the lower Forties. The cab turned West, drove past Sixth Avenue, and stopped in the middle of the next block on the south side.

"Stop right here across the way," said Limpeck in a high voice, "and let me off."

Gamadge obeyed. Limpeck scrambled out, and watched the cab drive away and Ashbury enter a dingy vestibule one flight up from the street. Then he came out from behind the car and followed.

Gamadge watched him leaping up the iron stair and jostling Ashbury in the vestibule. There were apologies from Limpeck, ignored by Ashbury. There was a wait. Then the door clicked open and they both went in.

Gamadge leaned out to look at the building. An Italian restaurant and bar in the basement, a theatrical costumer on the first floor, a manufacturer of theatrical properties above, and on the top floor curtained windows.

Limpeck came back and stood on the curb to talk to him: "The name's Smiley. Top floor. Only three residential flats, far as I make out, third and top back and top front."

"Gritty neighborhood," said Gamadge.

"I never cared for it myself, but it's convenient in a way. Eating places everywhere and the show business all over the neighborhood."

"I used to come over here or hereabouts to get myself costumes and wigs when I had to go to masquerade balls or be in private theatricals."

"Them was the days?"

"Them was the days. Thank Fortune they're over."

Ashbury came out and went into a bar on the left of the Italian restaurant. Limpeck said: "I'll go over and take a peek."

There was another bar not far from where they waited. Gamadge said: "That's a grill. I might get coffee and a sandwich."

"Why not? Stay near the door, though, in case he's getting a quick one."

Gamadge went into the bar and ordered his coffee and a cheese sandwich on toast. Presently Limpeck came across the street and joined him.

"Subject's having his lunch in there, and I think he's going to take his time about it. He's had a double Scotch and ordered another."

"Have something yourself on me?" Gamadge put down money and was about to call the bartender. Limpeck shook his head.

"Can't risk it."

"I'm going to risk a call on Smiley."

"You are?"

"Have to, yes. If Ashbury comes out before I get back, take the car and hang on to him if you can."

"He's good for ten minutes, I should think."

"I don't suppose I'll be long."

Limpeck said: "You relying on that big gun you got in your pocket? They'll see it right away."

"Don't care if they do."

Limpeck stood on the curb beside the car and watched Gamadge across the street and up the iron stairs, a look of doubt in his eye.

Gamadge pressed the Smiley bell. Presently the old door clicked, and he entered a hall that smelled of wet overshoes and mice. He climbed many stairs, found a door in the rear with *Smiley* on it, and rang. The door was flung open by a short, middle-aged woman who had once been a pretty woman. Beyond her Gamadge had a glimpse of an aquarium in a window, a birdcage above it, and afternoon papers on the floor.

The woman patted mahogany-colored hair, curled tight. She looked at Gamadge vaguely.

"I've just missed Ashbury," said Gamadge. "Awfully sorry to bother you, Mrs. Smiley."

Mrs. Smiley's prominent mahogany-colored eyes considered him without trust or acceptance.

"I want to get into touch with Mr. Bowles myself."

"Never heard the name."

"It's the name he's going under just now, isn't it? Wouldn't he prefer me to use it? I want to see him about Mrs. Spiker."

She stepped back, a deathly kind of emptiness on her face, and her eyes turned to the newspapers and back. He saw an unmade studio couch against a wall, an open suitcase on the floor, another smaller one beside it. "Smiley," said the woman, in a voice as empty as her face.

A fat man appeared in a doorway. He was in his shirt-sleeves; his features were small, his expression one of meaningless good humor. Some people might have thought he looked silly; Gamadge thought him formidable.

"Did you ever hear of anybody named Bowles, Gus?" asked the woman, who had moved a little aside and was now watching Gamadge's right hand. It was in his pocket, or half in; but Gamadge thought that Mr. Smiley wasn't perturbed by that fact. His long arms hung as if ineptly at his sides, and his silly smile did not change.

"Not that I remember," he said, in a low, gentle voice.

"Or anybody named Ashbury?"

"Not that I remember."

"There's some mistake," said the woman.

"I'm sorry." Gamadge backed politely away.

"That's all right." The fat man came forward a step or two. "You got us mixed up with some other parties."

"I must have. Nice cozy place you have here."

"Try to change apartments these days!" said the woman.

"In your place I shouldn't dream of trying." Gamadge had reached the hall. "Well, thanks," he said, "and let me apologize again."

He was still speaking when the door shut in his face.

Running down the stairs, he did not look unduly disappointed. He found that Mr. Limpeck had driven to the end of the block and around it, come back, and parked on the other side of Sixth Avenue, pointing North. Limpeck stood on the curb waiting for him.

"How you make out?"

"Not so bad."

Ashbury came out of the bar and walked towards Sixth; his face was lowering and his step lagged. Gamadge got into the car and sat well back, Limpeck stood on the far side of it. Ashbury did not even glance in their direction; he paused as if uncertainly, looking up the street. Then he crossed to the north corner, waited for the red light, and walked slowly to the other side of the Avenue. He hailed a northbound taxi and got in.

"And here we go again," said Limpeck, settling himself beside Gamadge. He concentrated on the cab ahead, which soon turned Eastward and continued in that direction until it reached Park Avenue. It then turned North again.

Limpeck allowed himself a cigarette. "Smileys home?" he asked.

"Yes. They say they never heard of Ashbury, Bowles or Mrs. Spiker. They're quite tough. Smiley waited to put on his gun before he came out to speak to me—he had it on his hip, I think. I shouldn't like to shoot it out with Smiley. I left."

Limpeck laughed tolerantly. "Too bad I couldn't leave Ashbury."

"Well, I didn't want to shoot it out. I found what I went for."

"You did?"

"Of course. Ashbury went there to find where Bowles is; they know Bowles, and I shouldn't be surprised if he spent last night there after he finally quit work. I think his suitcase is there, and Mrs. Spiker's may be there too."

"Say, listen," said Mr. Limpeck, "we ought to—"

"The suitcases are gone by now, Limpeck, and we have to stick to Ashbury."

"I can drive the bus. You get off and telephone them to send down and grab hold of those Smileys."

"Our assignment is Ashbury. You said yourself that it needs two for this kind of job."

"If Bowles is there that's more important..." Limpeck had his hand on the door.

"Bowles isn't there. Would they have opened up if Bowles had been there? They let me in as soon as I rang."

"Big Shot, I don't think you're handling this right."

"Don't get sidetracked, Limpeck. We've still got Ashbury, he doesn't know it, and where's he off to now?"

Mr. Limpeck took his hand off the door and sank back. He was dimly conscious of a change in the relationship between himself and his helper. The helper was the one who seemed to know exactly what he wanted, and to be doing it.

O.K. with me, thought Limpeck.

The end of the chase came in a quiet, expensive street between Park and Lexington in the Fifties, where big houses still stood behind handsome grilles, although there had been an incursion of small apartments and shops, a bar and a restaurant. Ashbury got out in front of a brick-and-marble mansion on the north side of the street. Gamadge stopped the car on the south side, farther down. Limpeck was out of the car and across the asphalt before Ashbury had paid off his cab.

Ashbury went up the low flight of marble steps, Limpeck loitered by. Ashbury rang and was admitted by a colored man in a white coat.

Limpeck came back to the car: "Asked for Mrs. Oldgate." He was staring. "Has he stopped trying? Just paying a call on a millionaire?"

Gamadge had descended and was looking at the house; then he glanced at the small walk-up beside it, where a little old man was sweeping out the vestibule. He said: "I've got to get in there, Limpeck."

"In where? Where Ashbury went?"

"Yes. I might get some information first from that superintendent next door."

"What if Ashbury comes out again?"

"You take the car and go after him."

"Listen, you said—"

"This is no sidetrack, Limpeck; the Smileys may have sent Ashbury here. I've got to get in. I haven't much time left for Ashbury anyway, I promised Nordhall to go up to the Park Avenue house at three o'clock, look after Miss Paxton's things and get the key from the cleaning woman."

"You mean you want me to take your bus for the rest of the assignment?"

"Certainly. When you get through with it, get somebody to leave it up at my place."

"If he don't go home after he comes out of here, I'll have him pulled in. If he ever does come out of there," added Limpeck gloomily. "You can't tell on these streets with these big houses—there might be a back way."

"All I want is to get in." Gamadge went across the street and wandered back past the little old man, who was nonchalantly sweeping dust into the corner of the sunken vestibule.

CHAPTER FOURTEEN

Second Call—Oldgate

THE SUPERINTENDENT of the walk-up, a dreamy little Irishman without many teeth, leaned on his broom when Gamadge spoke to him, and put a forefinger politely to his front hair.

Gamadge said: "I used to know this street pretty well once, when all the houses were private houses. Changes, here."

"And many everywhere. It was the zoning us for business did for us, sir; that meant the speak-easies came in. But we've quieted down since the liquor came back."

Gamadge leaned against the railing that enclosed a row of privet bushes. "Across the street," he said, watching while Limpeck drove to the Lexington Avenue corner and poised the car for flight: "that was Miss Fenson's house—the actress."

"Beautiful inside. And the two ladies next door to her, they put on those balconies. I took care of all the furnaces in those days."

"I don't suppose anybody knows the street better than you do."

"Not so well as I did. I only take care of this house now. And since the war, sir, you wouldn't believe what's happened to the little place. People doubling in the flats that used to be considered a tight fit for one."

Gamadge turned to look at the big brick house next door. "Do the same people live there still?"

"No sir, that old couple has gone. Brother and sister, if you remember, sir, nice old lady and gentleman. When she died he moved to the country, that was in the middle of the depression days, and a terrible time the agents had with the house afterwards, they couldn't rent or sell."

"Regular white elephant?"

"It was, sir, and at last they rented to a dressmaker. The other householders on the block, they were tired of seeing the doorway littered and the signs up, and they resigned themselves. Madame had a big opening with mannequins, and some of the householders went, and came away quite pleased." A half-smile appeared on the superintendent's wrinkled face. "But a year after, the patrol wagon came one morning and took the ladies all away."

"No!"

"And only the postman wasn't astonished. But the postmen know more than the rest of us."

"The house seems to have recovered."

"We don't know much about it."

"Don't you? What does the postman say?"

"He knows no more than the rest of us this time. They've been there these ten years, and the name's Oldgate; it seems like an old-fashioned kind of boarding-place."

"I hope the boarders won't go off some morning in the patrol wagon."

"I don't think so this time, sir; elderly people, some of them men."

"I might try there for a friend of mine."

"Well, sir, you might; but it's hard to get into any kind of a place just now."

"What's the proprietor like?"

"I've never laid eyes on the person, sir. But I'm seldom out on the street meself."

Ashbury came out of the house in question. Gamadge turned his back to light a cigarette. He offered one to the old Irishman, and gave him a light; then he went up the two steps to the pavement, watched Ashbury walking towards Lexington, and mounted the marble flight next door. He rang a bell sunk in a bronze rosette.

The colored houseman came promptly; a tall, efficient little mulatto with good manners. He said he would speak to Mrs. Oldgate, but he didn't think they had a vacancy.

Gamadge produced his card, and was ushered into the depths of a shadowy hall. The houseman disappeared through a curtain near the foot of a broad, winding stair.

The hall or lobby widened at the far end, and became a circular reception room with a high white fireplace. The dark-blue carpet, though a little worn, was still soft to the feet, and the furniture was heavy, solid, and designed to match the Empire style of the ceiling and walls. There must have been much gold on the white woodwork in the days of the old couple, but it had been painted over now; otherwise there could not have been much change. This background had certainly never been specially chosen for a type of person likely to be rapt away in a streamlined Black Maria.

An elderly woman in black was descending the stairs on noiseless feet. As she advanced Gamadge saw that she was wearing a shiny dark wig, and that she peered at him as if she could not see very well. Her black dress was long for the fashion, and over her stooped shoulders she wore a knitted cape of black wool.

She looked up at him from the card in her hand. "Mr. Gamadge?" Her curiously toneless voice was low.

"Yes. Mrs. Oldgate?"

She stood in front of him, quietly observing him, with

now and then a lizardlike movement of her head from side to side. Gamadge was unable to place her in any category of human beings known to him.

"Raymond said you were inquiring about accommodations for a friend."

The words were few, but Gamadge was now able to place Mrs. Oldgate geographically; place her, at least, south of the Mason and Dixon line. He said: "Yes, an old friend— an elderly man friend," and began to rack his brains.

"I am always very careful," said Mrs. Oldgate, "about references."

Gamadge had dredged up something, after desperate mental effort, that he hoped would do. "I heard of you," he said, "from Miss Botetourt." He gave it what he remembered as the regional pronunciation. "Old Miss Botetourt."

Mrs. Oldgate accepted old Miss Botetourt calmly, but her head swayed in negation: "I don't call her to mind. I suppose some friend mentioned me to her." The low voice died. She opened the black velvet bag that was hooked to her belt by a silver clasp, and extracted a box. From the box she took a lozenge, put it in her mouth, chewed it thoughtfully, swallowed it, and spoke more clearly: "I have a very choice clientele, very quiet people. They are particular."

Gamadge felt as though he were cradled in a vast calm, out of space and time, where hours were as days. He said: "That would suit my old friend Winterberry."

Mrs. Oldgate raised heavy-lidded eyes. "He could be quiet here."

"That's what he wants. A charming old gentleman," said Gamadge, who had begun to visualize Winterberry as an expensively dressed solitary with a hoary moustache— perhaps even a beard—who wore a fur-lined coat and carried a thick silver-headed cane.

By some telepathic method he had got Winterberry across. "Raymond is very good at valeting," said Mrs. Oldgate, "but of course he has not much extra time."

"Winterberry would bring his own man, of course. He's quite well except for a touch of rheumatism; the trouble is that he's been disappointed in his reservations for Biloxi."

Gamadge didn't know much about Biloxi, but he didn't want Mrs. Oldgate to think that Winterberry was a mere spending type who wintered at Florida resorts from pure lack of imagination.

Biloxi passed. "If it were for a short stay," said Mrs. Oldgate, "there might be a chance. We could make your friend comfortable. The table is very good, and the guests can be served with their own sherry and so on at table. There are pleasant evenings here, cards and music, but the guests can keep entirely to themselves if they prefer it. No criticism, no talk. Absolute privacy."

"It sounds pretty wonderful, Mrs. Oldgate."

"There's just a chance; one of the ladies is waiting for *her* reservations."

"Could I possibly see the room? You know how it is—I'd like to describe it to Winterberry. He's adaptable, but old people want to know what they're in for."

"I'm sure Mrs. Beaupré wouldn't mind; she loves company."

They went slowly up the winding stairs, Gamadge reflecting confusedly on the various and violently contrasted types of humanity that had climbed them in the past...On the first landing a little white dog rushed to meet them, yapping.

Mrs. Oldgate glanced over her shoulder at Gamadge. She said: "We allow animals."

"Good. Winterberry can't be separated from his brindled bull."

"We have a very responsible dog walker."

"Splendid. Such a problem in bad weather."

They mounted another flight, and went along another white-paneled, blue-carpeted hall towards the rear. Mrs. Oldgate tapped on a door, waited, and then put her head in.

"A gentleman would like to see the room, Mrs. Beaupré."

"Gentlemen always welcome," cackled a voice. They entered a large bedroom, comfortably furnished, with a coal fire in the grate and a large parrot cage in one window. Beside the other window an old lady sat in an armchair. She wore a flowered hat, a quilted dressing gown, and big gold bracelets. There was a robe over her knees. She was cozily surrounded by a strong aroma of Bourbon whiskey.

"Well!" she said.

"This is very kind indeed of you, Mrs. Beaupré," said Gamadge.

"Not at all. I'm trying on my new hat."

"Beautiful."

"It's a Mr. Gamadge," said Mrs. Oldgate, reading from his card.

The old lady gave Gamadge the most coquettish bow he had had in twenty years.

"If young gentlemen are startin' to come into this bo'dnhouse," she said, "I won't be in such a hurry to get down home."

"I shouldn't think you'd be in a hurry, Mrs. Beaupré." Gamadge looked from the vast mahogany bed to the padded chaise longue, from the sizzling radiator to the glowing fireplace, from the parrot in his cage to the cracker crumbs on the floor. "I should think you'd be too comfortable to move out."

"There's a private bath," said Mrs. Oldgate, moving her lizard head to the right.

There was, and a colored maid was puttering about in it.

"And the view is very pleasant; your friend would get the morning sun."

Gamadge went over to the parrot's window and looked out on a series of tended gardens, divided by low hedges and fences.

"The householders on the block put their gardens together at one time," said Mrs. Oldgate. "Of course there are fences now."

"But low ones. Very pleasant indeed." Gamadge studied

the layout; an alley ran from the last garden on the left between apartment houses, to Park Avenue.

"We get a few cats," admitted Mrs. Beaupré, "and that wakes up the dogs."

"But in the country," said Gamadge, *everything* wakes up the dogs."

Mrs. Beaupre cackled. The colored maid—she looked like a personal maid, she was so commanding of presence and yet so old—came in from the bathroom with a pile of undergarments. She went over to a wardrobe trunk in a corner and began to stow them away.

"High time for me to be leavin' this cold town," said Mrs. Beaupré, "and with travelin' what it is I ought never to have come North at all this year; but I can't miss my visit to New York."

"You stay on," said Gamadge, joining Mrs. Oldgate at the door. "Buy some more of those nice hats. I'll tell Winterberry you're here on a mission to gladden the heart of humanity."

Mrs. Beaupré's cackle of laughter was so nastily echoed by the parrot that even its mistress seemed taken aback; the colored maid looked at it as one retainer looks at another who has stepped out of line. Mrs. Oldgate, with something like a smile, ushered Gamadge into the hall and closed the door.

"Cheap at any price," said Gamadge.

"A hundred a week."

"Quite satisfactory."

"I'll let you know Mrs. Beaupré's plans."

"You know how to treat them."

"Only the best people," murmured Mrs. Oldgate, as they began the descent of the stairs.

Yes, thought Gamadge, and I bet the ones that haven't a hundred a week can come for less. All the Bourbon they want, and sleep it off afterwards. What a sanctuary for the elect!

A sanctuary; not only for the elect, but for those recommended to Mrs. Oldgate's mercy by the elect. That unreconstructed rebel would face down all the forces of law and order, the entire

Homicide Squad, if necessary, in their behalf. If necessary she could arrange a hurried departure by way of those gardens and the alley to Park Avenue. She could, and Gamadge thought she would. Any person who tried to get private information about her clients' affairs from Mrs. Oldgate was licked before he began.

There was only one thing Gamadge could do, and it was hardly necessary, but it would be a satisfaction; and it would be another fragment of evidence, evidence that he needed very much. As they began the descent of the lower stairs, he said: "I think I saw young Ashbury coming out of here, while I was parking my car."

She stopped, turned her head, and looked up at him; and he could see, positively see the image of old Mr. Winterberry, his fur-lined coat, his valet, his brindled bull, melt from her belief as a snow image dwindles in the sun.

She said, going on down the stairs, "Nobody of that name called today. Raymond?"

Raymond materialized from the shadows below.

"The gentleman is going."

Going for good, thought Gamadge, but he had his information. He turned at the open front door to make his farewells, but Mrs. Oldgate wasn't there.

A cab took him up Park Avenue. It was not quite three o'clock when he stood for the third time in less than twenty-four hours and looked up at the front of the Ashbury house. It was stark in the light of midafternoon, with its shuttered windows and its scrawled door, with the dust drifting up to its threshold. The iron rail of the balcony stood leaning inward, a little awry; it said in its own language: "Something terrible has happened here."

Gamadge stood thinking of what had happened until steps came flapping along the pavement, and he turned to confront the homely figure of the cleaning woman.

CHAPTER FIFTEEN

Closing Up

NOT WISHING TO RAISE the echoes of this desert neighborhood by shouting, Gamadge waited until the cleaning woman shuffled up to join him under the portico. Several patrons might have contributed to her wardrobe—the well-worn ulster that was too short for her, the brown cloth skirt that was too long, the large felt hat perched on top of her gray hair. From her grimy paper shopping-bag the heels of working shoes protruded.

"Well, Mrs. Keate," said Gamadge, "here you are on the dot. Glad you turned up."

"Turned up? It's my time for Miss Paxton."

"I mean I was afraid you might have seen the papers and stayed away."

"Papers?" The instant reaction of cleaning women to the unexpected—in any form—is defiance. Anything may be a threat, a threat of oppression, to the touchy ego of a cleaning woman. She stood eyeing Gamadge with reserve, both hands in their brown fabric gloves clutching the string handles of her shopping-bag.

"Poor Miss Paxton is dead."

"Dead!"

"She fell."

"My soul. Was it a stroke?"

"No, the fall killed her."

"Terrible. I did think she was quite an old lady to be here all alone by herself. Trip on the stairs?"

"No, it was a peculiar accident. I wanted to ask you—" Gamadge stepped back to look up at the balcony. "She fell from that ledge."

The cleaning woman also stepped back, stared up, and then looked at Gamadge. "From *there*?"

"And the railing gave. She evidently liked to come out on that little balcony; she came out there yesterday when I left, to see me off. You do remember me, Mrs. Keate? Remember my coming yesterday to call?"

"Certainly I do. My goodness." She looked up at the railing. "I've been out there myself. I swept it up."

"What I wanted to ask you was whether you noticed that the rail was loose."

"I never touched it—thank goodness. That's the most dangerous thing I ever heard of. Who'd be responsible?"

"In your case? Heaven knows. I don't know the law on empty houses. The owners, I suppose, unless there's accident insurance."

"I never heard of anything so careless—to leave a railing loose!"

"Well, of course it was only for ornament. Nobody's supposed to use that balcony."

"Work people have to."

"That's so."

After a pause during which she seemed to ponder the damage in dollars that she might have caused the Ashbury family, she asked: "I'm not wanted any more, then?"

"You're wanted very much today. I'm—my wife's an old friend of Miss Paxton's. They want me to close up the house and get her things packed up to send home. And to pay you, of course. Could you help out on the closing up and the packing?"

She considered it. "I could if it wouldn't take too long after five. I have four places a day, and by five I'm ready to quit."

"No wonder. We ought to get through it in two hours, I should think. Let's go in."

She got a key out of a large shabby handbag which hung in safety between her person and the shopping-bag, its handle over her left wrist. "You might take this now," she said, "before I forget it."

"Thanks." Gamadge inserted it into the keyhole. "Where did Miss Paxton get it—this extra key? Do you know?"

"She got it from the agents when they gave her hers." The cleaning woman followed him into the dark hall, and stood while he closed the door after them, shutting them into silence and a gray twilight. "I knew this house before," she said. "I cleaned for Mr. Ashbury. Of course there were servants then. After he died and the household broke up I left my key with the lawyer. And now I'm leaving it again."

"Miss Paxton told me what a convenience it was, getting someone she could trust."

"It was a kind of an accident. I was going by from my one o'clock place up the Avenue and I saw that the house was open. I had two hours free in the afternoons between three and five, one of my families went South for the Winter. I stopped in to inquire, and Miss Paxton engaged me right away. Only a couple of weeks ago, but I feel as if I'd known her longer. Such a nice lady. It's sad."

"It is sad. Suppose we settle up the money question here and now, Mrs. Keate."

"I might be a little overtime," she said anxiously.

"I'm going to ask you to accept a couple of dollars extra anyway, for your special job of sorting and packing up, and for the accommodation."

Mrs. Keate adopted the proper look and tone of reluctance; but she accepted the couple of dollars over and above the three dollars owing her for the Monday and Tuesday, and the dollar-fifty to be earned that afternoon.

"Now let's see," said Gamadge. "How do we go about this? I'll go over the house and lock windows and turn off the furnace."

"I'll do any picking up there is since yesterday, and strip the bed and put the laundry together; and put out the garbage."

"What about a laundry?"

"She had Campbell's, around on Lexington."

"I'll call Campbell's." Gamadge made a note.

"We can put the bundle down by the front door. There's never much garbage, Miss Paxton used to give it to the man next door in the mornings."

"We'll leave it out front today, the dickens with it."

"That's the man for you," said Mrs. Keate with dry amusement.

"And when you get all that out of the way," said Gamadge, "I'll help you sort out Miss Paxton's things. I suppose she had a trunk?"

"There's one in her bedroom. She always left it open. I'd like you to come up and look around for any valuables she had. I don't want to be responsible."

"She had none—only what she was wearing at the time of the accident."

The cleaning woman hesitated midway up the stairs: "What time—was she laying there long, sir, before they found her?"

"Last night. Not long."

"Might have been robbed!"

"Wasn't."

She went on upstairs. Gamadge opened a door on the right and entered a room with barred windows fronting on the street. It contained a huddled collection of furniture that included a sewing machine, and had probably been the servants' dining and sitting room.

Gamadge poked about, uncovered the sewing machine, opened closets. He went back to the laundry and kitchen, opening drawers and cupboards on the way. In both the back rooms he continued his search, even peering under the stationary tubs and among the cooking utensils. No portable flat surfaces here of the proper size and dimensions. It occurred to him again how few such implements are in general use. He fastened windows and the yard door.

He went down to the cellars; no portable flat surfaces there, not even a leftover coal shovel of any size.

He switched off the furnace, locked up, and went upstairs. In the front hall he examined the mosaic flooring; not a flaw or a crack for fluids to settle in, and the mosaic looked well scrubbed.

On the first-story landing he paused to listen; the cleaning woman was in the pantry beyond Miss Paxton's chosen sitting room. He went to the front drawing room and searched it, but found no detachable flat surface nor any practicable chair leg. In the book-room he stood and shook his head at the books; no book could have been used to strike that killing blow; hadn't the weight for it, and there was no purchase. He opened all the tip-out cupboards and ran his arm down to the bottom of them; could hardly get his arm down, so closely were they packed with their contents.

He heard the cleaning woman go upstairs, and went back to Miss Paxton's room to search it and the pantry. There was a bronze paperweight on the table, but it was round and hollow, like a muffin tin.

He gathered up all the things that looked as if they were, or had been, Miss Paxton's—knitting bag, spectacle case, writing case; he picked up the golf cape from the back of the chair and hung it on his arm. Then he went up to the second story, left his hat and coat on the stair rail, and entered Miss Paxton's bedroom—the large, dark, handsomely furnished room that had been Mr. and Mrs. Lawson Ashbury's. Miss Paxton's open wardrobe trunk stood in a corner. The cleaning woman was rolling up laundry in a sheet.

Gamadge dumped what he carried on the bare mattress of the four-post bed. The cleaning woman came out of the space behind it and saw him. She said: "I'm going to clean up the bathroom now, and then I'll be ready to pack. Those going in?"

"If you can get them in." Gamadge was wandering about, hands in pockets. He opened the closet door. "Not much here; she was wearing her coat when she fell."

"Nice-dressed old lady."

"I thought so too." He took the laundry bundle out into the hall and rolled it down the stairs, following it when he heard the telephone.

He picked up the receiver. "Oh, hello, Limpeck."

"Thought you might like the end of the story."

"I would. Very nice of you to call up."

"He came back home. Been kindly requested to stay there. Miss Vance has gone for a walk, she's got a very nice well-dressed cop trailing her. He's keeping up close, but she's just strolling along. I left your car in front of your house like you said."

"Thanks very much."

"They want me at the theatre when Miss Ashbury comes out."

"Do they?"

"She might pay some calls too. I got them to send down to talk to the Smileys."

"That's right."

"How you coming, up there?"

"All right. Nobody's been here since last night, so far as I can make out."

"What would they go there for?"

"I don't know."

"Well, hope to meet you again."

"Thanks."

Gamadge went up to the top floor. Servants' rooms, a trunk room with empty trunks in it. He came down to the third floor, where he found a back and a front bedroom, nicely furnished, a bathroom and some linen cupboards. Nothing like a portable flat surface in any of them.

When he returned to the second story the cleaning woman was at work in the bathroom, which was between the two bedrooms on that floor, and windowless. He went into the front bedroom, a kind of bed-sitting-room with a broad, sofalike couch in it. He put on the light, and then stood staring down at something that stood against the baseboard behind the door.

There it was, with its slender handle, its weighted shell-shaped base; he bent and picked it up by the fixed ring at the end of the twelve-inch stem, and swung it up and down in a murderous arc. He examined it closely; a fine old brass doorstop, eighteenth-century work, with an iron foot, and a smooth piece of iron clamped into the ornamental shell. The whole thing looked clean. The iron behind the brass was no rougher and no smoother than the pavement two stories below.

Why should it be in this room, which looked like a guest room? Gamadge opened and closed the door, and found that it had a loose latch. Easier to keep it shut with a doorstop than to have the latch replaced.

He put the portable flat surface back where he had found it, locked the windows, put out the light, and went back to look in on the cleaning woman. She was putting things into the drawers of the trunk; Miss Paxton's modest wardrobe was heaped on the bed. He went downstairs, picked up the laundry bundle, and turned. Iris Vance was standing in the doorway of the drawing room, looking at him.

Against the dusk behind her she had her ghostliest look; but presently she became less startling to Gamadge's eyes, a conventional figure enough in her dark-green suit and her neckpiece of reddish fur; a moderately pretty girl, as astonished by the sight of him as he was by the sight of her.

He asked: "How did you get in?"

"Jim lent me a key."

"He had a key, had he?"

"His father gave him an old key to the house, in case..."

As she did not go on, Gamadge finished the sentence for her: "In case the young people had business here?"

"Well, they were in town. They might..." Again she stopped.

"Might decide to come and see Miss Paxton after all? Why did *you* come, Miss Vance?"

She glanced about her vaguely. "I didn't hear anybody. I thought the house was empty."

"There's a cleaning woman upstairs. We're closing up, she and I. That's what I'm here for. What about you?"

"I came to look for that picture."

"Picture?"

"The one you thought was stolen."

Gamadge dropped the laundry bundle and straightened to gaze at her. "You think it's here after all?"

"I always thought Miss Paxton must have been mistaken about it. Mistaken this time, I mean—since she came."

Gamadge turned this over in his mind. "You mean the proof impression had been taken out of the frame for some reason, taken out of the frame by Mr. Lawson Ashbury, and the letter proof substituted? Why?"

"I don't know why. Perhaps he might even have meant to have it framed properly; to give away."

"Give away? To his son? To Mr. James Ashbury?"

"Anything makes more sense that the idea that it was stolen."

Gamadge, his eyes fixed on her, was biting the side of his thumb. At last he said: "That future sister-in-law of yours has persuaded your young man that you did steal it? Is the engagement still on, Miss Vance?"

"Of course it is."

"Why didn't they take you along and introduce you to Miss Ashbury's young man and his family, then?"

She turned away from him into the dark of the drawing room. "We weren't telling anybody about the engagement. You know that. We were waiting for Mr. Ashbury."

"And Ashbury couldn't spend the afternoon with you because he had to pursue Mr. Bowles."

She said, as if she hadn't heard him: "I did see the picture in one of those drawer things in the book closet; when I was a child."

"Great heavens, a little candor at last!"

"I wondered if the other could be there now."

"And what an idea that is." Gamadge came past her into the room and switched on lights. "Will you credit me when I confess that I haven't looked myself? But miracles do occur."

She came into the book-room after him. He put on the light, and tipped out cupboards. At the second one he paused and smiled. "Here we are."

"You haven't looked."

"I didn't look before. I'm looking now. You don't see it?"

"No. How can I?"

Gamadge gently drew the proof impression out by one corner. He held it up admiringly. "Beautiful. So clear and bright, so superior to the other one—that's the thing to say, you know, whether we see any difference or not." He slid it back into place among the others, and turned to look at her. "Did you really dare hope that if you found it here they'd believe you?"

"Believe me?"

"Believe you didn't bring it back just now and put it there. It *could* have been rolled under your coat and you thought the house was empty. Don't you really know how I found it before I saw it properly?"

"You couldn't see it at all. There are too many others packed in."

"Not packed in. Look again. Don't you see the edge—that it's been rolled?"

She bent to look, stared up at him.

"This copy's been rolled, as I rolled the other to bring it to your apartment last night. It's been out of the house."

She stood with her back on the woodwork, her hands on the shelf below the books; her eyes on his.

"And I can tell you something else about it," continued Gamadge. "It's been replaced since I glanced into these cupboards yesterday. Today I wasn't noticing—I shouldn't have seen it; but yesterday I should. Do you think Mr. Lawson Ashbury ever rolled this picture?"

She said nothing.

"But exactly when was it replaced? Between the time I went home yesterday and the time the murderer left here last night? After that the police were here until late. And after that—"

"After that," she said, "we were watched."

"Yes. From six to nine yesterday, or this afternoon; that's the choice of times." Gamadge turned out the book-room light and came into the drawing room. "Evidence—it's dangerous some-times, a two-edged sword. Be careful with it."

Standing in the doorway of the book-room she looked at him desolately.

"You ought to have brought a witness along with you, you know," said Gamadge. "Then you'd at least be clear for this after-noon. That well-dressed cop I hear you've trailing along with you—you might have brought him. But no, the last thing you'd do would be to use the police. What a mistake you're making."

"You don't know anything about it." She spoke almost angrily.

"But I'm allowed to guess. That's what I'm really here for—to guess, Miss Vance. I was even glad to help out with the closing up, but I was even better pleased to have a chance at recon-structing Miss Paxton's murder. Would it interest you—to listen to the reconstruction of a crime?"

CHAPTER SIXTEEN

Reconstruction

SHE CAME SLOWLY FORWARD. Gamadge pushed a yellow satin chair up to the hearth.

"I suppose," he said, "that this is your old friend."

"Yes." She touched its rounded back. "I remember it very well."

She sat down in the yellow chair. Gamadge brought a little table across the room, placed it beside her, and looked about him. He got a hideous little Worcester dish from the top of a cabinet and laid it on the table.

"Never meant for ashes," he said, "but we'll desecrate it. Smoke? No?" He got out matches and knelt at one end of the fireplace. "We'll see how much of an optimist I am. Miss Paxton didn't use the gas range in the kitchen, and she would never have asked them to turn the gas on for the sake of open fires; but Mr. James Ashbury may have sent instructions. He seems an openhanded kind of man; showed her consideration after her death—why not before?"

He turned a little wheel, and then applied a lighted match to the asbestos logs. Blue flames popped up and spread.

"Horrible things." Gamadge stood up. "But useful in an emergency. The furnace is off, and we should soon have felt a chill." He moved to her right, leaned his shoulders against the high mantel shelf, and looked down at her. "Not good manners to stand over you," he said, "but this is going to be a kind of lecture. There's a moral in it; but need I state it?"

She sat back looking at the blue flames, her feet crossed and her hands on the arms of the yellow chair. "I suppose," she said, "you mean I know who the murderer is. You mean I ought to have told."

"And that if you had told, Mrs. Spiker might be a live woman at this moment, instead of a labeled corpse in the morgue, with half her face shot away?"

She said, her face expressionless, "I don't know anything."

"You've got me quite wrong, Miss Vance; I'm not going to insult your intelligence with platitudes. My moral applies only to murderers."

She glanced up at him and away.

"There are two ways down to murder," continued Gamadge, lighting a cigarette. He dropped the match in the Worcester dish, and went on: "And one way is the safe way. Miss Paxton's murder was so well-planned and so brilliantly executed that it couldn't go really wrong; the murderer had a straight path down to victory. Safety down there, satisfaction and peace of mind—for somebody who could breathe the air and didn't mind the dark.

"But this murderer couldn't resist what looked like an amusing little detour, a tempting excursion into another and pettier sort of crime. But it wasn't a detour after all, it was a road through hazardous country to a very different place. And even now the murderer doesn't know it; thinks it was as safe as the other, and will end in that dark, peaceful cave.

"A chance in a million that Miss Paxton had ever noticed that pale old aquatint among all the other pictures on the wall; the murderer took the chance. It's the kind of thing," said Gamadge reflectively, "that makes your flesh creep. It's as if Macbeth turned out Duncan's pockets first. No great tragedy here, of course, but a great intelligence at work, stooping to small larceny. Murder for profit, and a little extra on the side. Perhaps no more than a gesture of arrogance or contempt? Murderers can't afford them.

"What was the result of this one? Miss Paxton had to be killed that very night, so that she wouldn't talk to others about my theory of a substituted engraving; I had to be killed—I'm sure you know why—and when my murder didn't come off, Mrs. Spiker had to be killed before she could talk to me.

"But still the murderer thinks there's a straight safe road down to that infernal, quiet cave."

Gamadge dropped ashes into the Worcester dish, and went on:

"Much has happened since I saw you last night, and you will already have gathered that I'd had enlightenment. But I could do with more, and you can supply it. Would you supply it if you could see these events, not from the personal angle, but from that of the humane being who has the build-up? People read something or they hear something, and it doesn't make a sharp impression; they say: 'I don't want the gory details.' But it's the gory details that count; it's the gory details that drive peace-loving persons like me into action, against instinct; even against the instinct of—er—self-preservation.

"To make a beginning, I have found the weapon with which Miss Paxton was killed."

The girl's hands moved on the yellow satin of the chair, and closed tightly.

"The police," continued Gamadge, "would soon have found it; I merely got here first. If they didn't get here first it was because they made two reasonable assumptions—either (as was more probable) the murderer brought the weapon along and took it away afterwards, or else the murderer left it here, and wouldn't return for it. Why return for it, especially to a house that might be swarming with policemen?

"So the police didn't hurry a search of this house, I searched it myself just now, and having found the weapon I could make a more or less satisfactory reconstruction of the crime.

"The murderer must have visited the house at least once before that fatal visit last night; to discover that the iron rail of the balcony was loose, to loosen it still farther, to plan the whole campaign. It is obvious that the murderer possessed a key. The visits could be made by day or night without Miss Paxton's knowledge—she was rather immobilized in her sitting room, or in her bedroom up above, by her disinclination to climb stairs.

"We come now to the murder itself. An appointment was made with Miss Paxton by telephone, made after I had telephoned to her shortly before seven o'clock. She mentioned no such appointment to me, and if she had made one she would surely have mentioned it. The murderer telephoned as late as possible to prevent just such a possibility. Someone was coming to call at nine o'clock.

"At approximately nine o'clock, then, Miss Paxton is in her sitting room working at her letters. You didn't feel much sympathy for her when *you* called on her; but to me she is a sympathetic figure, innocently working away. She is waiting for the doorbell to ring. It rings, and she goes down and opens the front door.

"I'm inclined to think that at first she saw no one."

Miss Vance lifted her white face to look at him.

"I don't think," explained Gamadge, "that the caller would have cared to be seen clearly by a passer-by, and would therefore be standing in shadow—against the side of the portico. Miss Paxton opens the door; a well-dressed person steps forward into the light from the hall, and with a word of greeting goes straight past Miss Paxton and into the house. The front door is closed, the visitor turns.

"Miss Paxton may have had time to wonder why the visitor was carrying a longish parcel, loosely wrapped in newspapers. I say newspapers because—as you know from my own activities last night—people do carry the last editions about with them when they wouldn't carry another sort of bundle.

"But I don't think Miss Paxton had time to wonder about the newspaper parcel, or about anything else; since from now on the action becomes rapid, very rapid indeed. Let us imagine that the visitor drops something to the mosaic floor—something like a bunch of keys, that would make a noise. Miss Paxton looks down at it. In that moment the paper wrappings drop away from whatever the visitor is carrying, something heavy swings up and down, Miss Paxton sinks under it as if she had been poleaxed.

"Instantly the weapon—a curious, long-handled thing which I believe to have been wrapped in something waterproof, like a fragment from a thin raincoat—the weapon is set down; a purple woollen scarf is whipped out of the murderer's pocket, and is wrapped tightly around Miss Paxton's head and neck. To keep blood from the mosaic? Not entirely for that reason, in fact not principally for that reason, since the mosaic can be washed—will be washed. No: for technical reasons which I won't go into now. Accept the fact that it had to be used, just as Miss Paxton's coat had to be found and put on her, instead of the golf cape which she wore for short outings and kept near her in the sitting room.

"The weapon is taken upstairs to Miss Paxton's bathroom, which is windowless and can be lighted up. Always safer, you know, not to put lights on and off and allow people in the rear to see them and compare times afterwards.

"The weapon is examined for bloodstains, but there are none under the waterproof wrapping. I didn't tell you what it was, did I? It was a brass doorstop, broad at the base, and the brass shell of the base weighted with a smooth, fitted piece of iron. It made the kind of wound that Miss Paxton would have received if she had fallen from the balcony to the pavement. It belongs here in the house, in a bedroom whose door has a loose latch; but I have another reason for thinking that it belongs here: the murderer would never have used an unusual weapon that could be traced, and such things often can be traced to the original owner or purchaser.

"But why, you may ask, take the thing away, a heavy thing like that, only to bring it back again on the night of the murder? Why not leave it in some convenient place downstairs, in those closed rooms where Miss Paxton obviously never went? Because the murderer would have had no excuse to go alone into those rooms, or elsewhere; and Miss Paxton had to be kept near the front door, and in the hall, where the flooring was washable.

"There are materials for cleaning and washing, I have no doubt, in Miss Paxton's bathroom. They were brought downstairs, and the mosaic carefully scrubbed if it needed scrubbing. I don't think it did.

"Everything was replaced, or wrapped up to be carried away. A stamped addressed letter was brought down and put in the pocket of Miss Paxton's coat; that was an extra touch, not necessary. People go out for airings at night, even when they have no letters to mail."

His eyes met Iris Vance's again.

"We might pause here," he said, "to ask ourselves whether our pickpocket murderer hadn't brought the portrait of Lady Audley along too, wrapped around that doorstop, under those newspapers. The best, perhaps the only chance to restore it to one of those tip-out cupboards. The murderer might have had your idea—that if it should be found in that tip-out cupboard, as it surely would be found, my whole theory of a theft would be proved false."

Iris Vance asked faintly: "But what good would that do—to anyone but me?"

"Miss Vance, the police would rather not make trouble for that nice Mr. James Ashbury of San Francisco; they would be very glad to find some way of avoiding trouble. They'd like to be able to believe that a holdup man was on your stairs last night, that the same holdup man, fascinated by whatever Mrs. Spiker had in her handbag, followed her to the Hambledon and then to my place and murdered her with a thirty-two calibre pistol. They'd like very much indeed, if they could, to believe that Miss Paxton's death was an accident after all.

"But you know what I'm prepared to say about that portrait of Lady Audley in the tip-out cupboard."

She said: "You think now that I did it all."

"There's always that nasty little hitch, though; why, after I came trampling into the picture with my telephone call to you, should you have gone on with the murder scheme? The police assume that if you'd known the murder was coming off last night you'd have dropped the scheme or stopped it. But we mustn't waste time theorizing now; we must get on with the murder scheme, which has arrived at the moment of great risk. But was it so great? A matter of three minutes at most, I should say, and a clear view up and down the avenue for blocks.

"The murderer had to go out on the balcony, push down the railing, and retreat, leaving one of the old doors open. The risk consisted in the chance that someone would pass and see the open door and the flat railing while the murderer was still in the house. But the murderer had reconnoitred first, and wasn't in the house afterwards for long. Just a minute more to turn off the hall light, place Miss Paxton's body on the street where it was found, shut the front door and walk away, up- or downtown. One more minute to turn the corner—then safety.

"And if anybody came around a corner before the murderer got there, what was to prevent the murderer from giving the alarm? 'I've just passed somebody who seems to have had a stroke or a heart attack.' The newcomer goes to look or to get help, and the innocent bystander melts away.

Innocent bystanders often do—they hate being mixed up in street accidents and giving their names and waiting for the ambulance or the police.

"Now tell me, Miss Vance: do you think the whole thing, from the murderer's arrival to the murderer's exit round the corner, could possibly have taken more than a quarter of an hour?"

Iris Vance had sunk back into her chair; her eyes were closed. She did not reply.

"Not more," said Gamadge. "The only thing that took any time at all was the washing up—everything else was a question of minutes. As for Mrs. Spiker—no need to reconstruct that murder. Did you know that she was shot down at my door? I wish you had seen her."

Iris Vance rose suddenly, turned away from him, and went blindly towards the dark hall. She was halfway down the stairs by the time Gamadge had found the switch on the landing. He was about to turn it when she stopped; the front door had opened.

Gamadge had a moment's glimpse of a silhouette against the dusk of the street—a big, hunched figure, a blur of face lifted, a hand gripping the knob. Then the door was pulled shut and the hall was empty.

Iris Vance was clinging to the stair rail. She looked up and back at Gamadge, horror in her eyes—for he was smiling.

"What a lot of keys there must be to this house," he said. "Even Bowles got in. But he wouldn't stay, didn't like the look of us. I shan't run after him without my hat; and your man won't, he has to stick to you. But why should we run after him? He's all washed up now, poor fellow. Miss Vance—no— don't *you* run after him!"

But she was gone, and the door swung to again.

Gamadge went up to the next story, got his hat and coat off the rail, and went in to find the cleaning woman. She was ready for the street, pulling on her long-fingered gloves.

"All done, Mrs. Keate?"

"Yes, sir. Here's the trunk key; I got everything in, but you'd better look round. Was that the laundry man? I can feel it when the front door slams."

"No, I haven't called him yet."

"The garbage was so little I put it in a paper bag. I could throw it into a rubbish can on Lexington."

"That's an idea."

"And there's a little food, not much. It's in a carton."

"Too much for you to take home with you as a favor to me?"

"No, sir. Thanks."

They went downstairs; she paused on her way into the sitting room and looked up at the wall: "Wasn't there some kind of picture up there yesterday on the faded place?"

"Yes. Miss Paxton had me take it down for valuation."

"Poor old lady, I guess the work was too much for her."

She went through to the pantry and came back with her bundles clasped in both arms. Gamadge said: "Here, that's too much; let me—"

"No, it's all right. I'll soon get rid of the paper bag with the garbage. Don't forget the laundry, sir."

"I'll attend to it tomorrow."

"Thanks for the extra money."

"You certainly earned it."

He opened the front door for her and closed it after her. Then he stood in the dark hall, almost in an attitude of listening; but there was no sound in the empty house.

CHAPTER SEVENTEEN

Down

THE CLEANING WOMAN slapped along on her flat-soled brogues from the Ashbury house to the next corner south, across Park Avenue, and on to Lexington. There she got rid of the bag of garbage in the rubbish basket, and then stood waiting for her downtown bus. Others waited with her; men with their chins sunk into their collars—for a chill breeze had come up from the East River—women with their handbags clasped against them for fear of pickpockets. This was the going-home hour, but the heaviest traffic was North to Harlem and the Bronx.

The bus came at last, lumbering down the avenue and swooping to the curb. A few passengers left it by front and side doors, and the waiting crowd climbed on. Mrs. Keate had her nickel ready, dropped it into the box and pushed in. She snatched a handle midway to the exit doors as the bus lurched on.

A late-comer had jumped aboard as the doors began to close; he too had his collar up and his hatbrim down, and yet he didn't try to join the warm huddle further in. He remained up front, quite deaf to the exhortations of the driver, until people shoved past him to get off at the next stop. When they had gone he did move along, caught hold of a handle, the first on his left, and stood swaying; every now and then he bent over a little to peer out at the street numbers as they went by.

Mrs. Keate had worked herself into a seat near the exit doors, next to a window; she sat looking out at the gray streets, settled with her belongings on her lap as if for a considerable journey. The bus jogged on to the Seventies and through them, stopping at every fourth corner, stopping for red lights. Still crowded, it jogged on through the Sixties.

In the middle Fifties it stopped once for a light, and the cleaning woman rattled impatiently at the exit doors. The driver opened them at last for her, and she got off. She hurried to cross the Avenue in front of the bus before the light changed.

The man up front had not tried to get a seat. Now, peering out as he had continued to do, he had a glimpse of the cleaning woman as she scurried by. He came to life, elbowed his way to the front doors, and again just made them.

Traffic had started up and down the Avenue by the time he got to the curb, but he crossed at the risk of life and limb. The cleaning woman was plodding along towards Third Avenue; he plodded behind her, head down and shoulders hunched. They crossed Third, went on to Second, and crossed it. In the middle of the next block she turned to climb the steps of a rooming house.

The man paused twenty feet behind her and stood looking up and down the street. It was one of those streets that have either been half reclaimed from decay, or arrested on the way there. Neat walk-ups were on either side of the rooming house, and a fine modern apartment house on one corner.

He went into the vestibule of the walk-up nearest him and waited there.

The cleaning woman meanwhile had entered the rooming house with a key. As she advanced towards the bleak stairs a stout woman came from an open doorway on the right.

"Well, Mrs. Keate," she said, "you're a little late this evening. Bus tied up?"

"Oh, good evening, Mrs. Jensen. No, I was kept overtime."

"I was waiting to see you and say good-bye; in case I was out when you left tomorrow morning."

"I'm glad to have a chance to say it again. I'm sorry to move. It's a nice quiet house, and cheap for a place with cooking privileges."

"Well, if you get on with your relations, that's the nicest way to live. Did you say your sister-in-law is in New Jersey?"

"Yes. Near Newark. I don't know; it'll be quite a trip to work."

"Well, we can't have everything. I bet your customers were sorry to lose you."

"They were real nice about it."

"Well, we're all square. Good-bye, and I hope to see you again sometime."

"I hope to see you. Good-bye."

The landlady withdrew into her room. The lodger went slowly up three flights to a top floor rear room, which she unlocked and locked after her. This was her fortress, a cold little sliver of a place partitioned off from its neighbor, where she was her own mistress. The occupants of rooms like this did their own cleaning; they had no extra money to pay out in tips to colored maids at Christmastime.

She sidled along between bed and dresser to the window, and pulled down the shade. Then she dropped her parcels on the bed and turned on the light. She stood looking quietly around her, pushing back wisps of hair.

Downstairs the front doorbell rang. It was answered after a while by a colored woman in a blue denim apron, her hair tied up in a checked dishcloth.

The man with the pulled-down hat stood in the vestibule. He asked: "Mrs. Keate live here?"

"Top rear."

"Insurance."

"Step right up."

"Thanks."

He mounted through the silence of a respectable house. Workers were relaxing before they went out again to eating places for supper, or assembled materials to be cooked on the gas rings in the hallway kitchenettes. When he reached the top floor he did not knock at Mrs. Keate's door; he listened for a few moments, and then retired to the stairs. He sat there, hunched up in the dimness. One thing about a top floor, there was no through traffic.

The cleaning woman had dragged a suitcase from under the bed—a small, cheap case, empty. She gathered up a few plain articles from the top of the dresser, a heap of plain clothing from inside it, and put them into the suitcase. She flung her shopping-bag on top of them. There was nothing whatever in the shallow closet beside the door, but she made sure. At last she took off her felt hat, rammed it into the suitcase, and snapped down the lid.

The carton of crackers, coffee and sugar from the Ashbury house she left open on the chair under the window; there was no table.

The room was now ready for its next occupant—bare and neat. She put her purse under her arm, picked up the suitcase, and turned out the light. She unlocked the door, left the key in the lock, and went out into the hall, shutting the door behind her. Nobody would come near the place until the landlady decided to climb the stairs next day or the next.

Just outside her door, on the left, was another; it opened on a ladder to the trap in the roof, and the ladder was surrounded by fire hazards—brooms, mops and pails. She stepped up on the ladder, dragging the suitcase, shut the door after her, and climbed to the trap. She unbolted it and pushed it aside. Shoving the suitcase out on the roof, she scrambled up and out herself, and replaced the trap lid.

Picking up the suitcase, she walked across a low parapet to the next house West. This, the neat walk-up, had a shed over its trap door so that the cover could be left up in Summer even on rainy days. The trap was not fastened. She climbed down, closed the trap after her, and descended this ladder. At the foot of it she stood in darkness listening, then opened a door and looked out into a well-lighted hall. It was a nicely decorated hall, white and gray, with a glass wall bracket and a gray carpet.

She went directly across the hall, and unlocked a door. She entered a room, walked to one end of it, let down Venetian blinds, and then turned on a shaded lamp.

Bright chintzes here, a long mirror between the windows, a marble chimney piece, modernistic furniture, an upholstered day bed at the other end of the room, near the door. She dumped her suitcase on the day bed, shook off her ulster, and went directly into a spotless kitchenette. Nothing in the icebox but ice and oranges, but she only wanted ice. She got a bottle of Scotch out of a cupboard and made herself a stiff highball. She lighted a cigarette, and returned to the living room with the glass in one hand and the cigarette in the other.

She drank some of the whiskey, smoked half the cigarette, and then set the glass down on a stand, and the cigarette on the edge of an ash tray beside it. She opened the door of a large closet, which contained nothing but a fur coat, a small hat, a black dress, a pair of black suède pumps, and a big, handsome traveling case. She dragged out the case, opened it, and placed it on a chair.

She fitted the other suitcase into it; then she pulled off her dress, her draggled slip, her stockings and the brogues.

She was now clothed in foundation garments of the finest materials and the palest pink.

She packed the traveling case with all her discarded clothing, finished her highball and the cigarette, and walked across into a bathroom. She ran a tub of hot water, bathed, scrubbed her face and neck with soap and afterwards with cleansing cream, dried herself briskly with a rough towel. She put on the rose-colored undergarments, and then went into the living room and got sheer stockings and a pearl-colored slip out of a drawer. She put them on, and put on the suède pumps.

She went back into the bathroom and worked on her face with cream, powder, lipstick and rouge; manicured her hands, painted her nails, and brushed back her hair. When she had dressed it and applied brilliantine it looked neat, fashionable and cared for.

Looking at herself in the bathroom mirror she saw a striking if not handsome woman in her forties, with narrow eyes; prematurely gray-haired, clear if sanguine of complexion, with purplish shadows under the eyes and—in spite of the lipstick—a thin line of mouth. The lipstick could not disguise the width and lack of contour there. The bright eyes were red-veined, the whole face predatory. But she was pleased with it. She went back into the living room and emptied the dresser drawers, turned the old purse inside out, transferred its contents to a black suède bag.

She got the things out of the closet and put on the dress—a short, plain, smart affair that made her look even taller and slimmer than she was. She clipped on a pair of gold earrings and a pin to match. There were rings in the suède bag—she did not put them on.

She sat down on the day bed, then got up again to make herself another highball. She came back and sipped it, looking relaxed and happy.

Presently she got up again, put on the little black hat in front of the mirror, went out and tapped on a door at the other end of the hall.

It was opened by a shorter, plumper woman, dressed very much as she was, and looking as highly groomed. They exchanged smiles.

The shorter woman said: "Well, Mrs. Brant! What a stranger! I never see you. Do come in."

"I'm so sorry, but I haven't a minute, Mrs. Ferris."

"I know how you traveling people have to rush. I don't know how you stand it."

"I'm used to it. I like it. You real estate people could tell us buyers something about rushing; you're always on the go. How lucky I was to get a broker that actually owned a house herself. I love my little place."

"You don't get much good of it."

"You've been wonderful about subletting. And now I've come to break the news to you—I'm giving it up for good."

"Oh, don't say that!"

"They've changed my territory. I'll be in the Middle West."

"But everybody has to come to New York to do business!"

"Don't tell them that in Chicago!"

"And you've only been here about two weeks."

"There's one thing, you won't have much trouble in getting another tenant."

"Oh, I could rent overnight. You needn't worry about your lease."

"Well, anyway, this month is paid up; and I'd like to leave something for cleaning expenses, if there are any, and a tip for the superintendent. I paid the maid."

"You've always been wonderful about business; but then you're a business woman." Mrs. Ferris took the ten-dollar bill. "Where shall I send you word about the lease and so on?"

"I wonder if you'd just write care of general delivery here; my plans are so uncertain. They'll get instructions where to forward mail."

"There's certain to be a refund for you; I'll deduct the brokerage charge, and send the surplus on."

"Thanks so much. I simply hate to give the place up. It seemed a fearful extravagance, just for a few weeks in a year, but 1 had to have a place to come to."

"And we always sublet for you from May through October."

"Well, good-bye, Mrs. Ferris, and good luck."

"The same to you. Have you much stuff to move out?"

"Nothing that won't go into my bag."

"When are you leaving?"

"Tonight. I'll be out of this in a couple of hours. I'm going to Boston tonight."

"I don't know how you stand it!"

"Oh, my itinerary is all fixed for me, you know. I don't have to worry."

"Well, I'm awfully sorry. Be sure to stop in on me at the office when you're back in town some day."

"I certainly will."

They shook hands cordially. The landlady retired, closing her door; the tenant went back along the hall. She had entered her own flat and was about to close the door behind her; but a hand came over her shoulder and held it wide. Her head jerked around; if she had not been clinging to the knob she might have fallen.

Gamadge put his hand on her elbow. He said: "Sorry I had to startle you."

She put her other hand on the knob and violently shook the door, as if in a senseless effort to dislodge his grip on it. He said: "Don't do that, that's the way Mrs. Keate would act."

"What do you mean? Who are you? Get away. Let go of me; my name is Brant. How dare you?" The breathless voice was kept low.

"And that's the way Mrs. Keate would talk. She'd go on saying 'Some mistake'; go on saying it forever. You ought to know, you've made a study of the type. Have you played the part too long?"

"I tell you I don't know what you're talking about." She had recovered herself a little, was standing upright, and facing him. Her skin under the powder and make-up showed mottled, streaked with angry red.

"This is a waste of time," said Gamadge irritably. "Senseless. Am I likely to let you lock me out now, after I took all the trouble to follow you downtown and over the roofs? I might have been held up for a while, too, if I hadn't been guided by the noise of this trap door falling into place. I know what you call yourself, I was listening on the stairs out there. Let's go in and shut the door; you don't want your landlady in on this, do you?"

She stood silent, her long fingers working at the clasp of the big suède handbag.

"Get yourself another drink," said Gamadge. "You need one. I can't get it for you, not while you have that gun. And I don't want to wrestle with you for it, or shoot it out with you, either. I have a gun of my own this time. Go and get yourself a drink, and then sit down on the day bed. Let's see whether you won't end by throwing me your little gun of your own free will."

She turned her head stiffly from side to side, then let go of the doorknob and turned away.

"That's right," said Gamadge. "Let's have our talk while there's time. There's not too much time, I think, Mrs. Ashbury."

CHAPTER EIGHTEEN

Basic Fears

AT THE NAME she paused. Then, with her back to him, she asked harshly: "Time for what?"

"For me to make up my mind about something. Before Bowles gets here. He can't be far behind us."

At the name she cringed, and Gamadge, watching her, looked suddenly interested, suddenly surprised. But she pulled herself together and went into the kitchenette, Gamadge close behind. She picked up the bottle of whiskey and came back past him with it. She sat down on the day bed, poured a great splash from the bottle into the glass, and drank it off neat. Gamadge returned to the door; he closed it, and leaned up against the side of the frame. She sank back with closed eyes. When she opened them she looked different—cold, competent, alert.

"What business is it of yours," she asked, "if I try to win a bet?"

"Is *that* your defense?"

"I don't need one. People will back me up."

"You mean poor Ashbury?"

"I tell you it was a bet. It was a joke. He wouldn't come East to look after his own property, and I said I'd come to see whether this old lady, Miss Paxton, was honest and capable. Some people—rich women, too—think nothing of taking commissions from dealers. It was my idea—to pretend to be a cleaning woman. That was the best way to watch her. The rooming house, the whole thing, was my idea. James didn't like it, but he'll back me. I soon found, of course, that Miss Paxton wasn't going to take graft; so I was going home."

"You keep this flat for holidays?"

"Yes, of course I do. I've had it for years. James approves. Everybody has to have *some* private life."

"Mr. Ashbury knew about this flat?"

"He didn't know where it was. Lots of people have some little place where they can go and not be bothered by telephones and letters. Everybody needs a rest cure now and then. They'd go crazy without one."

"You've led them an awful chase, Mrs. Ashbury; for some reason they've been trying hard to find you. Bowles nearly caught you last night after you tried to shoot me on the stairs outside the Vance apartment, but I suppose you wedged that ladder in the fire exit up against the door, and had a chance to get away from him."

"What are you talking about? I never was at the Vance apartment."

"No, you were in San Francisco. Why did Ashbury's butler have orders to pretend you were there when Nordhall telephoned your husband last night? To protect your privacy while you were on your private cure?"

"Of course. They never told when I was away."

"Why did they want to find you this time?"

"I didn't know they were looking for me. I suppose it was on account of Miss Paxton's accident. I read about it this morning, and I was greatly shocked."

"So were the Ashburys and Bowles and Mrs. Spiker. They were so shocked that Bowles disappeared, and the Ashburys couldn't get in touch with him. Tried to find him at an apartment belonging to some people named Smiley, and then tried to get news of him at a Mrs. Oldgate's. Bowles would inquire there for you, evidently. Are you from the South, Mrs. Ashbury?"

"My mother's family came from the South."

"You stayed at Mrs. Oldgate's in other days?"

"Everybody knows we all—all my mother's people— always stayed at Mrs. Oldgate's when they were visiting in New York. I haven't seen her for years; I don't even know where her place is now."

"Bowles is a private investigator employed by your husband?"

"I never heard of anybody named Bowles. My husband wouldn't employ a private investigator to look for me."

"Not even if he wanted to find you very much? The whole family's here to look for you, and they let in another relation on it—a Miss Vance. And of course poor Mrs. Spiker."

"I never heard of—"

"You've simply been on vacation, and impersonating Mrs. Keate the cleaning woman in order to watch the activities of Miss Paxton?"

"Yes, and if you make any scandal about it you'll regret it to the last day you live."

"There's been too much fear of scandal in your family, Mrs. Ashbury. The young Ashburys and Bowles and Mrs. Spiker were to find you and get you home without scandal— somehow they had a lead on you this time, some clue to your hideaway. When Miss Paxton was killed they knew who'd done it, but their only desire was to get you out of it without scandal. Bowles and I have been neck and neck, but *I* didn't want to save the Ashburys from scandal; the question was, who should catch up with you first."

"That's nonsense. I was going home myself."

"They were afraid you mightn't be able to manage it, with me so anxious to prevent it. Well, I caught up with you first, but Bowles is right after me. He must have traced you to this street, after the shooting on the Vance stairs last night; but I suppose the Keate disguise and the two houses baffled him. He traced you up to the Ashbury house this afternoon, though; he was there, but when he saw me he vanished. His presence would give the show away—to me."

"I don't believe he was there!"

"You don't even believe there's any such person. He hoped I hadn't guessed the identity of the cleaning woman, and by Heaven I almost didn't. Not until this afternoon. I was pretty nervous alone in that house with you—pretty careful; but I was more or less banking on the hope that you wouldn't shoot me while we were alone together, and perhaps known by the police to be alone together there. While I was talking to Miss Vance in the drawing room, I stood with my eye on the door to the hall and stairs, and I had to talk for your benefit as well as for hers. *Did* you listen, I wonder?"

"If you were so sure of yourself," she said with a furious, baffled look, "why didn't you say all this up there?"

"Not for worlds. Now I have you in your own person— or is this another disguise too?—with Mrs. Keate's outfit in that suitcase at your feet. And I couldn't give you any cause to suspect that I knew who you were; if I had, you'd have put a bullet into your own head. That's why you hung on to the thirty-two, in spite of the fact that you've been leaving bullets from it all over the place. But how could you know that you wouldn't have a chance to get rid of it with the Keate identity? If I'd been in your place, though, I'd have left it in that rubbish basket with the garbage."

Leaning back again, her eyes half closed, she was a painted scarecrow—ageless and lifeless.

"But you felt so safe," said Gamadge. "And but for my obstinacy, you *were* so safe. Even now Bowles wouldn't have caught up with you; he'd have bungled over those two houses until you were gone, and you were going immediately. He won't bungle this time, because I left the trap doors open behind me."

Suddenly she sat up and slung the handbag across the floor. It landed at his feet.

"That's right." Gamadge stooped and picked it up.

"Get me out of here," she said thickly, "before he comes."

"I'll take care of him. Just tell me one thing, Mrs. Ashbury: why in the name of everything that's ridiculous did you ever take that proof before letter of the aquatint?"

As she said nothing, he went on: "You brought it back this afternoon under the cape of your ulster; but too late, much too late. It started all the trouble. You realized that, of course, when you hung about yesterday afternoon and heard Miss Paxton talking to me about it. You couldn't retrieve that error; it wasn't in order to retrieve it that you listened in on my telephone call to Miss Vance, and went to her apartment and waited for me in the fire exit; I know that. That's not why you tried to kill me."

She was looking away from him as if she had lost interest in what he said.

"You don't kill people for any such foolish reason as that," said Gamadge. "You have the wider vision and the long view. I must die because I was probably the only living person—Miss Paxton being dead—who had ever seen you in the Ashbury house. You went there at a time when the furnace man next door wouldn't, when there wasn't a chance, you thought, of any stray visitor. Miss Paxton knew no one. I was the great surprise. I was the only one who might at some future time meet Mrs. James Ashbury, or see her picture, and remember the Mrs. Keate who stood aside for me to pass on the Ashbury stairs.

"For perhaps Mrs. James Ashbury, when she's at home, doesn't look so unlike Mrs. Keate as Mrs. Brant the buyer does."

Still she was silent.

"Why did you take that Holbein engraving, Mrs. Ashbury?" Gamadge asked it almost plaintively. "A hundred thousand dollars—your very life—at stake, and you commit an act of almost pathological greed. You took it on Monday morning, I suppose? Because Miss Vance had been there the day before and could be blamed if anybody did notice a difference?"

She poured another inch of whiskey into the glass and drank it. "Yes," she said, "I took it on Monday morning. I didn't know there was anything special about it, apart from its being a proof before letter. My husband never said it was supposed to look like anybody, I don't believe he knew." She turned her head and looked at him, a bitter look. "Pathological greed? You don't know what you're talking about."

"Perhaps I don't."

"It's not greed to try to protect yourself from poverty and slavery and misery. It's not greed to try to be sure of three meals a day, a roof over one's head, heat in Winter and fresh air in Summer, decent clothes, security for one's old age. I was brought up comfortably, I wasn't trained to do anything. I had to make a living without knowing how, without ability or desire to work. I was a schoolteacher—you can imagine the kind of school, and the salary I got.

"I taught the things you can make up yourself or learn in a minute from some book. I walked the creatures, and looked after them like a nursemaid. Was it greed for me to marry that dolt James Ashbury? As for that engraving, apart from the fun of taking it after I found the other in that book place, I knew where I could sell it in San Francisco. I didn't get too much pocket money, you know."

"I suppose not," said Gamadge.

"But I was to have all the Lawson Ashbury money, all of it, in trust. That was the least James could do for me after losing his business in that stupid way. Jim can take care of himself, and the girl was sure to make a good marriage. She's going to make one—those Fredericks are rich.

"Then we got that ghastly news about the will—a third of the money gone for good, another third tied up perhaps for ten years, more; and nobody knowing how the fund would be administered or what would happen to money by that time. A bank is going to take care of that fund—was going to. My father lost everything he had when banks failed once, and he killed himself.

"A hundred thousand dollars? That's all I was getting, and it isn't enough nowadays."

"So you came East to collect another hundred thousand." Gamadge stated it in flat wonder.

"She was old. She'd never had money. She didn't need it," shrieked Mrs. Ashbury.

There was a violent pounding on the door. Gamadge opened it and stood in the entrance; Bowles confronted him, looked past him at the woman cowering against the cushions of the day bed, and looked at Gamadge again. He said: "Thanks."

CHAPTER NINETEEN

Showdown

"**Y**OU MIGHT PUT AWAY that gun," said Gamadge. "I have hers."

"That's good." Bowles dropped his gun into his pocket. Gamadge stepped aside to let him into the room, and closed the door on the blank and stunned countenance of Mrs. Ferris the landlady.

Bowles stood looking at Mrs. Ashbury, feet spread and hands in his pockets. He still had his hat on, and he needed a shave. Presently he turned and looked at Gamadge over his shoulder. He said: "I wouldn't have said 'thanks' to you two hours ago."

"You'd have come on into the house uptown, I suppose, instead of disappearing like a spook in a movie."

"I was still working for Ashbury then. Now I'm working for myself. I ducked over to Lexington to get away from that dick who was after Miss Vance, and I bought a paper. You wouldn't think I'd wait till five o'clock in the afternoon to buy an evening paper. I did, though; and I saw what had happened to my wife."

Gamadge said: "It's tough, Bowles. I didn't know myself that she was—I only guessed it a few minutes ago."

"My name's Mitchell. When I saw the paper I went over to the morgue—hell with Ashbury. I knew where this woman hung out, I could get after her later. I don't have to tell her what Mollie looks like now."

Gamadge said: "Easy, Mitchell."

Mitchell relaxed, took his hands out of his pockets and took off his hat. "Anything you say. She might have got away if it hadn't been for you, and she might have got rid of the gun. That fixes her." He turned to address Gamadge, his heavy face scowling. "I'll tell you what happened. Ashbury's a nice guy, I often worked for him in the past on business assignments, here and in the Far East. Mollie used to be an operative too, that's how I met her first, but now she is— was—in cosmetics, like Miss Vance said.

"Ashbury's had a tough time with his woman for the last ten years. She drank herself into sanatoriums, she picked up stuff in the house out there and sold it, she had him crazy. He's a conservative guy himself, and he had his children to think of. No knowing what she'd do next. He covered up for her all right, but until this time he never could find out where she went on her regulars; every now and then she'd disappear, and he was half out of his mind.

"This time he got me on the job, and Mollie too, and the young people—Miss Ashbury's going to be married, they were all scared out of their lives that this woman would make some kind of open scandal this time.

"I went through wastebaskets and trash, and I found a torn memorandum of train schedules and reservations through to New York; Ashbury had the address of some boarding house her family used to stay at when they had money. You understand that the whole thing was undercover, all Ashbury wanted was to get her back home quietly; so that's all we had, the memorandum and the address—not another thing. The four of us came East.

"I had my first glimpse of her on that upper landing of the Vance apartment last night, after the shooting, and I didn't know what the shooting was about. I was in a daze. Of course there had to be some tie-up with you and that picture; when you brought it along we all wondered whether Mrs. A. hadn't been up to something. Miss Ashbury—well, she was too scared to think straight. Behaved badly, but she had this idea of keeping everybody's mind off her stepmother. Never liked Miss Vance much, didn't like that spiritualist stuff. Hoped Miss Vance would say she *had* taken the picture, and somehow square herself with you and get rid of you.

"Never mind now. I saw this woman leave by the fire exit, I grabbed up the shell from her gun and went after her. She'd wedged the door, but I got it open. Luckily I had my rented car on the corner, but I got blocked. Anyway, I saw her get out of her cab at this street, and she was dressed the way she is now. When I got into the street myself, she'd disappeared. I finally decided that I couldn't do anything down here until morning, and as I was sure she hadn't seen me at the Vance place, I thought I'd better hustle over and check out of the Lingard. I knew Mollie'd check out of the Hambledon—there'd be police inquiries after that shooting on the stairs. So I moved in on some friends of mine named Smiley; he's an operator I used to work with here in the East. Mollie'd be sure to get in touch with me there. The Smileys don't know a thing about the Ashbury business. They're out."

"They know your wife's dead, Mitchell," said Gamadge. "They had a newspaper." He added, as Mitchell stared: "Of course they knew you and she were going under other names. I saw that, but I didn't bother them much. I gathered that you were staying there; but I wasn't after you personally, I was after Mrs. Ashbury, and young Ashbury apparently hadn't found her at the Smileys'. I kept after him."

Mitchell, after a scowling pause, went on with his story: "Well, last night I didn't dare 'phone the Ashbury apartment, or the Hambledon either; but I called Ashbury in San Francisco. We couldn't say much. He told me about Miss Paxton's fatal accident, and we agreed it was an accident. I told him about you and the picture, and we agreed that sounded like something the Missis thought up. I gave him the Smiley number, and promised to keep him posted.

"Mollie called me at Smiley's from a drugstore after she left the Hambledon, and she was badly shaken up; she'd heard from the young people about Miss Paxton's adjourned inquest. She said she was going to hunt up a trained nurse she knew and stay with her, only she didn't have her telephone number; I was to meet her on Sixth and take charge of her suitcase while she located the nurse.

"By the time she met me she'd made up her mind to get out from under; she was dead sure this Miss Paxton had been murdered, and who by, and what for; Mollie wasn't the sort to help cover up for a murder. You'll understand me, though," and Mitchell's face wore a faint grin, "when I say that I had every right to reserve judgment. So had Ashbury."

"Yes," said Gamadge gravely, "I understand your points of view."

"And I had a duty to my client. But I didn't blame Mollie, and I didn't like her being mixed up in such a dangerous thing anyway. I made two suggestions, though; the first one was to blow the works to you, not to the police."

Gamadge looked inquiring.

"You struck me as an intelligent kind of character," explained Mitchell, "who could see around the thing and hand it to the cops better than Mollie could; and I didn't want her spending the night in the police station and held as a material witness and so forth. You could handle it; anyway, I hoped you could. You acted and talked last night as if you was somebody."

"Did I?"

"Not just a nosy parker. My second suggestion don't sound good. I said for her to leave me loose awhile, I'd like to try to find this woman and get her back to San Francisco and into her usual sanatorium—whiskey cure, that is—before the police caught up with her. The whole thing could be handled better if she was already in care of her own doctor, and in a place where they knew her as a—kind of an invalid."

Gamadge looked at Mrs. Ashbury. She sat with her fingers around her highball glass, though it was empty. Her eyes were vague.

Gamadge said: "I see the idea."

"Mollie saw it. She likes Ashbury too. She agreed that she needn't know where I was; and I didn't tell her where I'd followed Mrs. A. to.

"I took the suitcase back to Smiley's. How could I know that this killer here was waiting up at your place for another try at you?"

"*I* had the idea, Mitchell," said Gamadge mildly. "I went in the back way."

"The trouble was that I couldn't get it through my head why she was after you. She's no fool."

"Afraid of future identification. Only Miss Paxton and I had ever seen the so-called Ashbury cleaning woman, or heard that she claimed to have worked for Lawson Ashbury. There mustn't be a hint of suspicion against the cleaning woman, you know; one hint, and she was done for."

"I was a damn fool. Well, today I came back to this street and hung around and asked questions; didn't make any sense out of the answers. Everybody here had a regular lease, and nobody told me that a Mrs. Brant wasn't here much. I suppose they were used to the idea, took it for granted, since she was supposed to be a buyer from the Middle West.

"As for the rooming house, I couldn't get any satisfaction there; and if you knew Mrs. A. as well as some of us do"—he cast a malign look at the abstracted face against the cushions—"you wouldn't have thought she could spend much time in that dump. I suppose she never did spend time in it."

"They're pretty independent there, with their cooking privileges."

"Just a place to leave from and come back to, and a locked hall bedroom behind her. Well, I hung around; and about twenty to three this afternoon a cleaning woman came out of the dump and walked away from the drugstore on the corner where I was parked; walked West.

"That's when I got my only bright thought in the whole case. I'd already questioned the colored maid, and I'd found out from her that all the roomers including the landlady were out for the day. The landlady was visiting, the roomers all work full time.

"Then where did this character come from? I went back and had another talk with the colored woman, and it comes out that this Mrs. Keate only arrived two weeks and four days ago. That fits in. I didn't wait to find out anything more down there—I beat it uptown to the only place I could think of where she might go in daylight—the Ashbury house. What must have happened, I suppose, was that she went out early as usual to buy herself a paper and catch up on the personal news, sneaked back by way of the other house as usual to have a comfortable read up here, and so on; nobody'd see her at that time of day, or notice a cleaning woman if they did. Then later she went out again by way of the trap door and the rooming house to keep her regular appointment. The colored woman just happened to see her leave the first time—she has something better to do than check up on the lodgers, and I don't think she could put one and two together anyhow.

"Anyhow, the whole business began to take shape in my mind; a cleaning woman could have had a chance to change those pictures, and it would be just like Mrs. A. to pick up a little extra value if she could. A cleaning woman...

"And she could have called up in her own person and made an appointment to see Miss Paxton last night at nine. Miss Paxton would have been delighted.

"Today she might be going back to pick up something else.

"I went up there, and a cop was in a doorway opposite; I'd know one a mile off. I took a chance when he was lighting a cigarette, and started in. I saw Miss Vance on the stairs and you on the landing, and I ducked out. Bought my paper, saw the news about Mollie, and went to the morgue. Said there was a mistake, but I didn't much care whether I *was* identified; I wasn't.

"Back I came here to wait for the cleaning woman; got in next door, saw the open trap there and here, nothing to it."

Mitchell looked about him. "Telephone?" He strode towards one at the far end of the room, picked up the receiver, and turned to Gamadge. "Want me to ask for that guy Mollie told me the Ashburys said you work with? What's his name?"

"Lieutenant Nordhall. It would be simpler."

Mitchell sat down and dialed. He said: "I can't do anything more for Ashbury now."

"Too personal?" Gamadge regarded him with a certain sympathy.

"Too personal. With somebody of my own killed, I feel a little different about covering up a murder."

"You reserved judgment, you know, Mitchell."

"That's so." He looked at Gamadge. "You're a fair man."

As he dialed, Mrs. Ashbury spoke in a faint voice: "Mr. Gamadge…"

"Yes, Mrs. Ashbury?"

"It's true; I've been in sanatoriums, and I'm often sick, and sometimes I hardly know what I do."

"That's right," said Gamadge cheerfully. "That's the line of defense; and if I had been convinced by it, I'd have tried to get you back to San Francisco and into your rest cure myself. That's what I wanted time to decide before Mitchell came; but I'm afraid I decided that you're as sane as I am."

CHAPTER TWENTY

Too Close To See

NORDHALL FLUNG HIMSELF down on Gamadge's chesterfield sofa, put his feet up, and asked: "Where's the cats?"

Gamadge, who was working at his desk, made a cheeping sound. The all-yellow kitten bounded from nowhere, rushed around the room, avoiding Nordhall's outstretched hand, and disappeared again.

"Has some other engagement," said Nordhall. He clasped his hands on his chest and turned his head to look at Gamadge. "Here it's only Sunday," he said, "and you've lost interest in the Ashbury case already."

"Somebody's paying me for doing this."

"Nobody'll pay you for finding Miss Paxton's murderer. Poor Ashbury."

Gamadge put down his pen and turned his chair. "What's he like?"

"Very nice, probably nicer than he'd be if he hadn't taken such a beating. But I don't think he was ever a bad sort of guy;

his children are fond of him, anyway. He's settled down with them in their apartment, and he's been mighty nice about the Vance engagement. And the Fredericks are going to stand by. Anybody'd know they would, just to look at them. The Ashbury girl's ashamed of herself, but Miss Vance and young Ashbury won't tell on her—about her trying to put off the picture stealing on her future sister-in-law. I guess she was half out of her head with the family troubles. Hoped Miss Vance would take the blame, and that you'd be convinced and drop the whole thing."

"I must have shaken them up considerably that evening."

"You did." Nordhall looked up at Lady Audley's locked, indifferent face. "You going to claim that as a fee?"

"No; I wouldn't want it. I've seen the other one. I feel a little delicate about sending it to Ashbury. Don't know quite what to do with it."

"Give it to me and I'll stick it back in the Park Avenue house. Poor Ashbury, I wouldn't like to force it on him myself. He's had a horrible time these last years—fixed it so that people didn't even know she drank, pretended she was off with him while she was in sanatoriums, took the whole rap. Nobody's going to persecute him about trying to cover up for the murders; and who's to prove it anyway? The same goes for his children and Mitchell. After all, it was Mitchell turned her in."

"So it was."

"She'd have been out of that flat and on a train before he ever caught up with her if it hadn't been for you. Of course, Ashbury's going to hire every psychiatrist between here and San Francisco, but the money motive is going to bother them. If he only gets her into an asylum for life he'll be a happier man than he expected to be when he got here. I can't get over what a soft thing she thought she had; foolproof scheme, and the Ashburys wouldn't give her away no matter what they thought. What made you think of her?"

"Think of her? She was part of the background—probably had a family interest in the money. And you didn't like the conspiracy idea any better than I did; but if it was a conspiracy to cover up for somebody else—that made it different. But who else? Ashbury was in California. Nobody left but the delicate second wife.

"A Chinese butler implies that she's at home, but makes it plain that she won't be answering the telephone. Naturally I thought of Ashbury's later history then—his change of character, the long trips out of town with the wife.

"I had Mrs. Ashbury in mind, and she was firmly planted there by the time I got to Mrs. Oldgate's. Bowles and Mrs. Spiker were investigators, everything fell into place. But I never thought of the cleaning woman. She was out of focus—too close up in front of my eyes. You ought to have seen her, Nordhall—perfect."

"Well, when did she get into focus?"

"When I stood in front of the Ashbury house on Wednesday afternoon, and turned and saw her coming along the street towards me. I'd been worrying right along about why I should have to be killed; so had you. What kind of menace did I represent to anybody—including Mrs. Ashbury—that could be got rid of by murder? What on earth did I know, or had I known, that nobody else knew? And then it hit me: I'd seen this cleaning woman.

"This cleaning woman, if she weren't deaf and hadn't gone home at five o'clock on Tuesday, knew even before I telephoned to Iris Vance that Miss Paxton and I were interested in the Audley portrait. She knew I was going to see Iris Vance at ten o'clock. She might have heard Miss Paxton tell me that story about her having worked for Lawson Ashbury, a story that somebody might be able to contradict. She had better opportunities than Iris Vance had to hunt about the house, find the other Audley portrait, and change the two engravings. She could have returned the portrait on Tuesday night or on Wednesday afternoon.

"And since she was supposed to be deaf, she wouldn't have

to answer the door or the telephone at the Ashbury house, or get into contact with the outside world at all while she was there.

"And it ironed out that situation at the Vance apartment," said Nordhall. "Of course Mitchell would run after her if he saw her on the top landing."

"It cleared up everything. All I had to do was to keep her happy until five o'clock, and then follow her home."

"Of course I see why she came back that afternoon. Couldn't afford any questions."

"That was great nerve, wasn't it, coming back? But she brought the fatal little gun with her. I went up and down through that house like a rabbit; I was thankful whenever I saw her working at her job, I can tell you."

"Luck was against her, but she oughtn't to have given luck a chance."

Nordhall finished his cigarette and went home. Theodore came up a little later to say that a young lady was calling on Gamadge.

"No name?"

"Miss Glendower."

"Oh. Send her up."

Iris Vance stood in the doorway of the library facing Gamadge, who shook his head at her slowly.

"You can't blame me," she said. "Those poor, poor Ashburys!"

"I hope Ashbury won't have to spend all the Lawson Ashbury money on her."

"If he does, we'll take care of him. He's so nice, Mr. Gamadge. How could you go on at me so, trying to make me tell?"

"We're even. You rushed away on Wednesday afternoon and left me in the house alone with a murderess, and not a word of warning."

"I knew very well you knew who she was. Oh how frightened I was when Mr. Mitchell appeared and I realized she was Mrs. Ashbury; he could only be there for her. We were all afraid of her by that time; poor Mrs. Mitchell, when I saw about her in the papers I was going to beg Jim to tell—but he'd gone out to try to find where Mr. Mitchell had gone. And you—you laughed."

"Did I? Well, there was something grotesque about it— Mitchell popping in and out, you dashing out of the house in a panic, and that madwoman upstairs packing and scrubbing for dear life, afraid to omit a gesture of her part."

"You do think she's mad?"

"Figure of speech. I don't know. I don't know the boundaries of that world. So far as I can judge, she's legally sane."

"Jim says she used to be so attractive and amusing— such good company. They all liked her."

"It's bad. I'm sorry you had to be involved in it."

"You were awfully kind to me that night."

"Was I? Business, strictly business. But that's over—let's sit down and ring for Theodore to bring something or other, and I'll have the cats in."

**Other titles in the
"Henry Gamadge" series
available from Felony & Mayhem**

Murders in Volume 2
Henry Gamadge #3
ISBN: 978-1-933397-01-6

"New York at its most charming" (*New York Times*) is the setting for *Volume 2*, first published in 1941. One hundred years earlier, a beautiful guest had disappeared from the wealthy Vauregard household, along with the second volume in a set of the collected works of Byron. Improbably enough, both guest and book seem to have reappeared, with neither having aged a day. The elderly Mr. Vauregard is inclined to believe the young woman's story of having vacationed on an astral plane. But his dubious niece calls in Henry Gamadge, gentleman-sleuth, expert in rare book, and sufficiently well bred—it is hoped—to avoid distressing the Vauregard sensibilities. As Gamadge soon discovers, delicate sensibilities abound chez Vauregard, where the household includes an aging actress with ties to a spiritualist sect and a shy beauty with a shady (if crippled) fiancé. As always in this delightful series, Gamadge comes up trumps, but only after careful study of the other players' cards.

"Henry Gamadge may now be counted a regular member of that choice company of the best fiction sleuths."

—*New York Times*

The House Without The Door
Henry Gamadge #4
ISBN: 978-1-933397-35-1

Mrs. Vina Gregson should be sitting pretty. Acquitted of
murdering her husband, she has inherited all his money, and
can afford to dress in the height of 1940s style. Unfortunately,
her fashionable clothing and coiffure go unseen, and much of
her money unspent, as the Widow Gregson remains essentially
a prisoner, trapped in her elegant New York apartment with
occasional, furtive forays to her Connecticut estate. A jury
may have found her innocent, but Mrs. Gregson remains
a murderer in the eyes of the public, and of the tabloid
journalists who hound her every step. Worse, she has recently
begun receiving increasingly menacing letters—letters
written, she is certain, by the person who killed her husband.
Taking the matter to the police would only heighten her
notoriety, so she calls on Henry Gamadge, the gentleman-
sleuth earlier encountered in *Murders in Volume 2*. Known for
his discretion, Gamadge also has a knack for solving problems
that baffle the police.

"You'll have a hard time finding better reading"
—*New York Times*

Evidence of Things Seen
Henry Gamadge #5
ISBN: 978-1-933397-72-6

In the sticky summer of 1943, and with her husband out of town on war work, a secluded cottage in the Berkshires sounds just the ticket to the newly married Clara Gamadge. The resident ghost, a slender woman in a sunbonnet, merely adds to the local color, even with the news that the bonneted woman died just one year ago, in the cottage that Clara is now renting. It's all nothing more than a deliciously spooky game, until the woman's sister is strangled while Clara dozes in a chair by her bed. The only clue: Clara's panicked memory of a woman in a sunbonnet standing at the door. Happily, Henry Gamadge—that supremely civilized gentleman-sleuth—arrives in time to calm his wife and solve the mystery (though not without some stellar help from Clara!).

"Ingenious ... most readers will be completely fooled"
—New York Times

Nothing Can Rescue Me
Henry Gamadge #6
ISBN: 978-1-933397-88-7

In mid-1943, and up to his elbows in war work, Henry Gamadge is longing for a quiet weekend. But when a half-forgotten classmate requests assistance, Gamadge is unable to refuse the tug of an old school tie. The problem, says Sylvanus, concerns his Aunt Florence—rather less Auntie Em than Auntie Mame. A giddy socialite, terrified of Nazi bombs, Florence has moved her extensive household of hangers-on to the family mansion in upstate New York. But menace seems to have followed them, in the form of threatening messages inserted into the manuscript of Florence's painfully bad novel in progress. Several members of the household are convinced the messages are emanating from Another World, but the politely pragmatic Gamadge suspects a culprit rather closer to home.

"Deliciously back-biting characters, all gathered in an imposing mansion in upstate New York...a pleasure"

—*New York Times*

Arrow Pointing Nowhere
Henry Gamadge #7
ISBN: 978-1-934609-24-8

Take one grand house, stuff it with staff, and make it home
to several generations. If they send their sons to Oxford and
occasionally knock each other off, you've got a country-house
mystery, that classic of English crime fiction. But if the boys
are at Yale, odds are that you're reading a New York mansion
mystery — a genre largely invented by Elizabeth Daly. Henry
Gamadge, Daly's gentleman-sleuth, does make occasional
jaunts to the country, but now he's back on the Upper East
Side, receiving missives suggesting that all is not right at
the elegant Fenway manse. He will, of course, unravel the
mystery, but even more delightful than the solution is the peek
at what the *New York Times* called "1940s New York at its
most charming."

"Told with all the skill that Miss Daly has at her command, and
she has plenty"

—*New York Times*

The Book of the Dead
Henry Gamadge #8
ISBN: 978-1-934609-56-9

The hospital sees nothing to question about the death of the
reclusive Mr. Crenshaw, and it's not as though he had any
friends to press the issue. He did, though, have one casual
acquaintance, who happens to pick up Mr. Crenshaw's
battered old edition of *The Tempest* . . . and happens to pass
that book on to Henry Gamadge. Gamadge, of course, is not
only an expert in solving pesky problems but also an expert in
rare book, and his two sets of expertise combine to uncover
the extraordinary puzzle of Mr. Crenshaw, which began in
California and ended on the other side of the country, at a
chilly New England rendezvous.

"An absorbing yarn that holds up to the end"
> —*New York Times*

Any Shape or Form
Henry Gamadge #9
ISBN: 978-1-934609-72-9

World War II has subsided at long last onto the ash-heap
of history, but in mystery fiction it is eternally, blissfully,
about 1926, meaning someone's getting murdered at a
country estate. The estate in question belongs to the rich
and genial Johnny Redfields, and the guest-list features his
aunt Josephine and her two sullen step-children. Redfields
had hoped to broker a peace-treaty, but it's not looking likely,
particularly since Aunt Josephine has joined a cult, draped
herself in flowing robes, and changed her name to "Vega."
Also on the guest list is Henry Gamadge, happy to defuse
the tension by steering Vega into the rose garden for a casual
chat, and conveniently at hand when Vega, leaning winsomely
against a tree, is shot in the head by someone with really good
aim.

Somewhere in the House
Henry Gamadge #10
ISBN: 978-1-937384-04-3

The Clayborn clan has been waiting 25 years to divvy up
Grandmama's fortune, locked up by her will and in a small
room in the Clayborn mansion. Tomorrow The Room is to be
opened, and the Clayborns can't wait to get their fingers on
the old lady's reportedly priceless button collection. Harriet
Clayborn, who doesn't quite trust her family, asks Henry
Gamadge to witness the Opening of the Room, to make sure
there's no funny business. Gamadge agrees, and it's a good
thing this masterful sleuth is on hand: the Room has been
hiding something grislier than buttons.

"An exciting novel and an excellent mystery"

—*San Jose News*